MURDER
MOST
DISTRESSING

MURDER
MOST
DISTRESSING

Leslie Stephan

ST. MARTIN'S PRESS
NEW YORK

Design by Kingsley Parker

Library of Congress Cataloging in Publication Data

Stephan, Leslie.
    Murder most distressing.

    I. Title.
PS3569.T3827M8   1986   813'.54   86-3703
ISBN 0-312-55312-9

10 9 8 7 6 5 4 3 2

MURDER MOST DISTRESSING

chapter ONE

Sergeant David Putnam sat at his desk in the Hampford police station, assiduously clearing up the paperwork surrounding the theft of a garden gnome. The Hampford police station, located on the ground floor of the Town Hall, consisted of a long narrow room bisected by a wooden counter. The area behind the counter, which resembled a used-furniture depository with its collection of battered filing cabinets, table, chairs, and desk, was in fact the office for Sergeant Putnam and the department's two patrolmen, Everett Hewitt and Ted Deegan. The front half of the room was sparsely furnished with a scattering of plastic chairs and a water cooler. From this waiting room a door opened into the office of the chief, Leonard Henderson. A large county map was spread-eagled against the back wall from which a corridor, lined with lockers, led to a lavatory and a holding cell.

A soft breeze blew fitfully through the screen door and the open windows, lifting the lower edges of the clippings on the bulletin board above his desk and causing Sergeant Putnam to glance up and now and then proprietorily at the sunlit world beyond his cubicle. It was a wonderful day to go off duty at noon, and he anticipated with pleasure the Saturday afternoon's outing to Mumbo-Jumbo Wild Animal Farm with Barbara, the boys, and Jenny.

Amazing how much work he processed alone in the

office, free from Everett's continual cynical comments and Ted's belching, lip-smacking, throat-clearing body noises which were all the more distracting for being surreptitious. Chief Henderson had disappeared into his office at nine o'clock, firmly closing the door behind him, which indicated either a prodigious amount of labor or a short snooze.

The creaking of the wooden stairs outside the station brought Sergeant Putnam's gaze to the screen door just as it opened. For one wild moment he thought that his gnome had been transformed into flesh. The little person advancing upon him was short and bulgy and dressed in the elfish colors of red and green: funny little suede boots, a red cotton skirt with a drooping hemline and a slightly yellowed white blouse of the style required of parochial schoolgirls, unironed, and bearing a dribble of stains down the front which Sergeant Putnam, veteran father, identified as berry juice.

As she approached the counter, she quite disappeared, remaining lost to sight until Sergeant Putnam advanced from the opposite direction to find her contemplating the dingy walls of institutional tan, the warped chairs with their pitted chrome legs, the oil company calendar that forever hung askew. Then she turned and looked up and up and straight into his eyes.

"I'm Mary Lou Stockbridge," she said firmly, "and I would like to see Chief Henderson."

But this was a small-town station.

"Stockbridge?" Sergeant Putnam mused pleasantly, leaning on the counter. "Any relation to Mrs. Eunice Stockbridge of Lake Wickiwitchi?"

"She was my great-aunt."

"Was?"

"She died yesterday."

"I'm sorry to hear that. We knew her quite well, you know, her and her Buick."

2

Indeed they had. Old Mrs. Stockbridge had persisted in piloting her monstrous machine right up until the day last summer when she had drifted through a stop sign two inches in front of the bumper of Hampford's sole cruiser.

"It's about her that I've come."

"And I can't help you?"

It was said with a grin and Mary Lou responded. He was a kind-looking big man, she decided, with his honest freckled face, and she felt a little better about her visit. Her stomach had churned all the way to town.

"I'm sure you could help me," she replied graciously, "but then I would only have to repeat everything twice because this is a very important matter and I think your chief will have to hear about it."

"Then we'll go right to the top," agreed Sergeant Putnam. Moving around the counter, he rapped on the spouting whale nameplate labeled Chief Henderson and, opening the door, ushered Mary Lou inside.

Chief Henderson sat up with a jerk behind his reproduction colonial pine desk, liberally sprinkling both desk top and his navy blue tie with amber flakes of tobacco. He was a small, spare man with closely cropped gray hair who had been moving diligently and carefully toward retirement since the day he joined the force. Sergeant Putnam offered Mary Lou the reproduction colonial captain's chair in front of the desk, and having made introductions, retreated to a seat beside the overflowing bookcase from which vantage point he studied Mary Lou Stockbridge.

Had he but known it, Mary Lou was an amalgam of all of her parents' worst features concentrated into their one offspring, her father having bequeathed her the Stockbridge jaw—or lack of it—while from her mother she had received the moon face and splodgy nose of the Freys as well as a pair of weak eyes that loomed like distorted blue onions behind the thick lenses of her plastic-rimmed

3

glasses. A thick fuzz of blond hair covered her arms and legs like meadow grass, while the hair on her head, of an undistinguished darker shade, was chopped off casually at earlobe length. Having asked permission to smoke, she was now puffing rapidly at a Marlboro Light which she pinched between thumb and forefinger.

Well on the way to becoming an eccentric, thought Sergeant Putnam in amusement, and she couldn't be more than thirty years old.

Chief Henderson seemed mesmerized by her appearance. He puffed at his ever-present pipe and fussed with his paperweight, a piece of quartz from the bowels of Clammy Cave.

"Well, now, Miss Stockbridge . . ."

"I've come to make a statement."

"I see."

"About my great-aunt."

"A very spirited old lady," said Chief Henderson with feeling. "I am sorry to hear of her death."

"That's what I've come about."

"Oh?"

"My great-aunt," said Mary Lou, "did not die a natural death."

"Well, well, hmmmm," Chief Henderson mumbled, puffing furiously. "What makes you say a thing like that?"

To Sergeant Putnam, who knew his chief so well, his embarrassment was painfully obvious.

"If you are going to make charges like that, a formal statement must be recorded and signed in front of witnesses, you know, Miss Stockbridge," Chief Henderson said repressively, as though he suspected her of dropping in for a lark. His skepticism toward her allegation, Sergeant Putnam realized, sprang in large part from a generational bias. He was of an age group whose judgments depended strongly on stereotypes of outward appearance. He was unable to classify this strange little creature and was as much perturbed by his failure to relate to her as by her nonconformity.

Mary Lou appeared unconcerned with his discomposure; perhaps she always evoked this kind of reaction. In any case, she regarded Sergeant Putnam's notebook with wry amusement.

"Wouldn't a tape recorder be more efficient?"

"Certainly, Miss Stockbridge," Sergeant Putnam answered with a grin, moving toward the next room to fetch a machine. She had a lot in common with her great-aunt. "Okay with you, Len?"

"Go right ahead. Get a slide projector while you're at it. We'll look at my sunset series."

Clearly Chief Henderson regarded the visit as a farce, with a high potential for humiliation. It was all very well for Sergeant Putnam to play the fool, but a chief of police did not have the same latitude.

"My goodness, where shall I start?" asked Mary Lou, eyeing the tape recorder with some trepidation.

"Why not start at the beginning?" Sergeant Putnam answered jovially. "It's always better than starting at the end."

Thank God his kids had never heard him at his jolly best. But his approach was provoking the desired results; Mary Lou Stockbridge was opening to attention like a flower to the sun.

"Well, I guess the beginning would be two weeks ago when I came up to the lake with Graunty, Great-Aunt Eunice, I mean. I spend my summers with her at Pineacres and with Mrs. Stroud, of course; she does the cooking and her daughter, Annie, does the cleaning and Wayne, her son, looks after the gardens and drives the car now that Aunt Eunice has been grounded. Of course we have visitors but a lot of the time it's just Great-Aunt Eunice and me. But today is her eightieth birthday. I mean it *should* have been and that's why everyone came up yesterday, or Thursday night in the case of my parents. Uncle Malcolm and Aunt Louise arrived yesterday morning and then my cousin Lance and we all had lunch together. Then Aunt Eunice went up to take her nap and Uncle Avery arrived and Lance and I went down to the beach. . . ."

★   ★   ★

The Blossoms of God were dancing on the lawn, twirling and spinning in their tatty yellow robes, oblivious to the lapping waters of Lake Wickiwitchi. The thump of the hand drum, the nasal whining that accompanied the dancing of the Blossoms, drifted across the hedge of wild roses that separated lawn from lake, assailing the senses of Mary Lou Stockbridge and her cousin Lance Turnbull, who were sharing what was left of the beach of Pine-acres, as their great-grandfather had christened his summer home. The clear blue waters of Lake Wickiwitchi had turned murky in the years since Charles William Stockbridge had bought the southern end of this rippling Berkshire body of water and erected his turreted, Tudor-style monstrosity overlooking Butterfish Bay. Chemical fertilizers, leaching from neighboring farmland, were carried by streams and brooks to the sluggish depths of the lake to nourish the rampant growth of algae and water weeds. Cattails encroached upon the strip of sand from both directions and the dock extended into a garden of water lilies. Each spring old Mrs. Stockbridge engaged a team of local laborers to poison, beat, hack, dredge, and otherwise subdue these rambunctious weeds so that for one more summer Stockbridges could immerse their pale city bodies in warm silt.

"So where was this guy?" Lance murmured drowsily, rolling onto his back.

"Skulking around the grounds. I've seen him twice in the last few days."

Mary Lou reclined on a plastic chaise longue, smoking a small woman's pipe which she had acquired while traveling in Sweden. She was wearing white nylon shorts and a homemade halter top in the style of two beanbags; her pale flaccid skin remained impervious to the rays of the sun. Lance, stretched on a beach towel, dressed in swimming trunks, was so thoroughly a Stockbridge, with his narrow skull, rabbit teeth, sandy hair, and fair freckled skin that he might have posed for the original James who had left the Old World in somewhat of a hurry in 1641.

"So he's probably helping Wayne or something."

"By hiding behind the garage?"

"Hell, I don't know, Lou. What do you want me to do about it?"

"Nothing. I don't expect action. I merely made an observation."

Shutting her eyes against the glare of the June sun, she strained to bring into focus an image of the man she had seen only yesterday at the edge of the woods. He'd had a thickset middle-aged look to him, bald, or nearly so, dressed in a white T-shirt and jeans, hardly the stuff of romantic fantasies, which is why she tended to believe in his existence; in any case, the male figures tossed out by Mary Lou's unconscious were thin, sneering, aggressive individuals.

The tempo of the hand drum grew slightly frantic; the accompanying chant shifted into high gear.

"My God," groaned Lance, "do they ever stop?"

"They're Graunty's darlings," Mary Lou said, with a slightly malicious smile. "You'll have to get used to them."

7

*   *   *

"It's a goddamn circus," said Avery Stockbridge, morosely gulping his gin and tonic. "She ought to be certified."

He was standing on the terrace of Pineacres with his brother-in-law, the Reverend Malcolm Turnbull, Avery, lean and freckled, narrow-skulled and weak-chinned, in true Stockbridge fashion, Malcolm several inches shorter, many pounds wider, and a great deal hairier, the luxuriant growth sprouting from ears and nostrils hinting at a body covering as dark as a gorilla's. Avery, having only just arrived from Boston, was still in his city clothes, his suit jacket tossed across one of the terrace's wicker chairs, while Malcolm, with some hours' start, was wearing slacks, a sports shirt, and Mexican huaraches.

"I am quite convinced that Aunt Eunice derives the greatest pleasure in her declining years from annoying the rest of us," Malcolm commented in his professionally fruity voice. "Many old people tend toward eccentricity as the expression of their individuality as it were."

"Balls," said Avery roughly. "It's a power trip. She's got us dangling on the end of these legacies like a bunch of hooked fish. Now we have to wonder if she's leaving something to *them* and how much, and she knows we're wondering and she loves it."

"Is that what you're worrying about? The inheritance?"

"Oh, come off it, Mal. Don't play the professional Christian with me. Do you honestly think any one of us would come here otherwise? Would you?"

"I must admit the summons, er, invitation, did come at an awkward time," Malcolm confessed. "I had to give up a conference in Hartford on the cloud as a symbol of God. But Louise and I would not think of missing Eunice's eightieth birthday celebration."

"Not if you're smart, you won't," Avery agreed.

*   *   *

In the kitchen at the back of the house, the cook and housekeeper, Mrs. Stroud, was chopping vegetables in a wooden bowl, bringing the cleaver down viciously on shiny green peppers and gleaming white celery. She was a lean, dark, intense, brooding woman whose ancestors had served Mary Lou's forebears with the same combination of scorn and envy that present-day Strouds displayed toward present-day Stockbridges. Dinner for ten tonight, that was only the beginning. They'd expect the usual lavish buffet in the morning, half of it going to waste, and then Mrs. Stockbridge's birthday dinner, the hypocrites toasting the old lady's health while secretly wishing she'd drop dead. Mrs. Stroud's daughter, Annie, doubled as waitress; Mrs. Stroud's son, Wayne, washed the dishes. A few more Strouds might be in order tomorrow. She wouldn't put it past Mrs. Stockbridge to invite that bunch of loonies in their filthy robes.

chapter TWO

At half-past five Mary Lou padded noiselessly into the kitchen in her yellow rubber sandals.

"Looking for something?" Mrs. Stroud demanded, ungraciously hinting at Mary Lou's proclivity for between-meal snacks. Declining to reply, Mary Lou crossed the room, fished a doughnut from a china crock, and leaning against the counter, defiantly enjoyed it, while staring down Mrs. Stroud. She had pulled a T-shirt over the halter top, yellow, with the slogan, *The Sun'll Come Out Tomorrow*.

"If you've got nothing better to do you can carry this tray up to your great-auntie. She's been taking her nap."

Mary Lou bit into a second doughnut. Raspberry jam squirted over her chin.

"She wants time to dress and have her cocktail before dinner."

"I heard you, Mrs. Stroud. Those who fret, get," said Mary Lou. "One more luscious bite and I shall fly."

Pursing her lips, Mrs. Stroud shoved the tray into Mary Lou's hands. There was something wrong with the girl's head, that was her opinion. She could seldom make head or tail out of her utterances.

Mary Lou trod cautiously up the narrow back stairs. She was put in mind not infrequently of the unmarried aunts of colonial days who received the charity of a home in return for ceaseless humble acts of service. Not that

10

she was in exactly the same position, but there was a certain collie dog aspect to her life which she bore without resentment. It was only when she looked through the eyes of the rest of the family that she saw herself as "poor Mary Lou," inconsequential Mary Lou, the carrier of trays and runner of errands, frustrated, unattractive Mary Lou in whose presence sexual references must be censored, simple Mary Lou who went about her undemanding tasks at the bookstore and spent her summers waiting on her great-aunt. All too often she found herself behaving like a parody of her family's creation.

Even her admirable straightforward honesty had been perverted by those around her who regarded her candor as the equivalent of the attention-getting device of a child or, among the more psychologically astute, as a facade concealing feelings of inadequacy. Mary Lou's directness was often equated with that of her Great-Aunt Eunice, who was known as an outspoken woman, which she certainly was, but not a very perceptive one. She might say, "Avery is an alcoholic" or, of Lance's older brother, "Bryon is a pompous ass" and hit the nail on the head, but she could say just as dogmatically and entirely erroneously, "Henry has no sense of humor" or "Louise is a nitwit." She did, however, voice her opinion, right or wrong, confidently and loudly, which was a wholesome departure, to Mary Lou's way of thinking, from the Stockbridge tradition of evading distasteful situations with a conspiracy of silence. If nobody labeled Uncle Avery an alcoholic then he wasn't one, and if everyone believed he wasn't, then he never would be and the whole unpleasant business would take care of itself.

"Upsy-daisy," muttered Mary Lou, heaving herself and her burden up the steep stairs, built when servants were as common as flies. The tray was brass, from India, covered with a white linen place mat on which rested a white linen napkin, two Peek Frean biscuits on a blue willowware plate, a cup of tea, sugar bowl and creamer, all in the same pattern, worn thin and blurred with age. It was a pleasing tray and Mary Lou, passing a great sheaf of peonies thrust into a green glass vase on the table in the upper landing, rested the tray on the edge of the table, and gently disengaging a handful of petals, scattered them like mauve tears across the white linen.

Her great-aunt's bedroom was at the end of the hallway at the front of the house, overlooking the lawn and the lake. Treading carefully along the runner, which had grown ragged in patches, Mary Lou was diverted from her goal by a hiss from her Aunt Louise, who came darting out of the room that had been hers since girlhood and which she had shared with Malcolm Turnbull for the past thirty years. She was so typically Stockbridge in appearance that a description would be redundant.

"One of those Blossoms," she informed Mary Lou in an agitated whisper, "has been in the house again. The situation is becoming quite outrageous."

"Well, I'm not the palace guard," said Mary Lou. "As long as Graunty lets them in, they'll come."

"But do we have to stand by and allow it? I do not like finding strangers in the lavatory. I wonder if they have some kind of hold over her. That would explain a lot."

"Did you find one in the lavatory?" Mary Lou asked with interest, sidling past her aunt to her great-aunt's door. It was slightly ajar and she turned to push it open with her buttocks.

"Well, not actually *in* it," said Aunt Louise. "I glimpsed him on the stairs. The thing is, don't you see, that he *could* have been in it or anyplace else for that matter. It's a question of privacy and general hygiene."

"We'll chat about it later, shall we," Mary Lou said, making a mental note to avoid her aunt for the rest of the day. Backing into the darkened room, she set the tray on top of her great-aunt's bureau with its embroidered linen runner, the bedside table being cluttered with a variety of objects, including Aunt Eunice's lower dentures.

Aunt Eunice's room had been "done up" by Mary Lou's Great-Grandmother Edith and not disturbed in seventy years. The walls were papered in a yellowing silver and pink design of scrolls and feathers; worn hooked rugs in a variety of faded floral designs lay scattered on the oak floor and crocheted antimacassars were skewered to the arms and backs of the heavy dark chairs. The walls offered, in somber frames, a gallery of grim-faced Stockbridges who were real people to no one except Aunt Eunice.

Mary Lou crossed the room and opened the curtains, letting in the eager light of June, still bright in early evening. The lawn was clear of Blossoms; a flash of yellow caught her eye, disappearing around the side of the house, as the dozen or so young people filed homeward, a trek that took them down the private dirt road that circled the lake to the macadamized grandeur of Route 117, whose winding way they followed for roughly half a mile before reaching the former moccasin shop where they now dwelt.

Mary Lou turned back toward the bed and the tea tray; Aunt Eunice was asleep in her usual position, on her back, her head on two pillows, pink crocheted bedspread folded neatly at the foot of the bed. But the lower end of the light thermal blanket that covered her body had twisted around her legs and the top half was dangling a foot from the floor.

Goodness, thought Mary Lou. What was she fighting? Old age?

"Graunty," she said sharply, unwilling to be held accountable for cold tea. Impatiently tossing the trailing

13

edge of the blanket back on the bed, her hand brushed her great-aunt's bare arm and knowledge was transmitted instantly through the cold flesh.

"Graunty?" she said tentatively, testing reality. Graunty slept on, a caricature of vain old age, with her soured, sunken mouth, the imperious nose jutting skyward between rouged cheeks, gray curls escaping their restraining net. Bending somewhat self-consciously over the bed, Mary Lou laid her ear to Aunt Eunice's chest.

It was in this awkward pose, as she strained to hoist herself over the side of the high four-poster, shorts nipping into her crotch, fat white thighs aquiver, that Aunt Louise came upon her.

"For goodness' sake, Mary Lou! What in the world are you doing?"

"What does it look like I'm doing?" Mary Lou snapped in annoyance. "I'm afraid that Graunty has passed over and out."

"Oh my God," cried Aunt Louise, bursting into tears. "Eunice, Eunice," she called, rushing to the bed and chafing her aunt's cold hands. "Oh, Mary Lou, dear, go get your Uncle Malcolm."

Mary Lou was already on her way, trotting with a certain pleasurable self-importance down the front stairs and through the front hall to the terrace where her uncles were sprawled in wicker lounges, slapping mosquitoes.

"Tha's not a good joke, Ma' Lou," Uncle Avery told her, continuing to focus blearily on some distant wave.

"I don't believe she's joking, Avery. Are you joking, Mary Lou? She says not, Avery. I'll see for myself," Malcolm said, rising ponderously to his feet. Gravely he made his way to the staircase and as gravely he returned. Going straight to the telephone in the hallway, he solemnly dialed the number of the local general practitioner, Clint Pearson, while Avery, who had wandered after him as far as the bottom of the stairs, leaned on the newel post and gaped at him.

"I'm afraid, Avery," Malcolm informed his brother-in-law, while waiting for the call to go through, "I'm afraid that Mary Lou was right. Aunt Eunice is at rest."

"She's where?" demanded Mrs. Stroud, popping on cue through the kitchen doorway. Her hearing was phenomenal.

"She is at rest," Mary Lou answered, rolling her tongue lovingly over the euphemisms. "Aunt Eunice has gone to her reward; she has left us; she has passed on."

"Oh my God," said Mrs. Stroud.

Oh my God indeed. Mary Lou discovered that her legs were shaking, a reaction ascribable less to the sudden departure of that domineering old lady upstairs who had been rendered insignificant at one stroke (and being Mary Lou she appreciated the pun even in the midst of her bodily distress) than it was to confrontation with her own mortality, which was not a familiar theme at the age of thirty.

What a damned impersonal business, she thought, outraged, and went to find her parents. No one else would bother to inform them.

Henry Stockbridge, Louise's younger brother, and his wife, Ellen, occupied the smallest, darkest second-floor bedroom, an assignment whose symbolism was not wasted on Mary Lou. As she had expected, the room was empty. Even *her* parents would have sensed something amiss by now. She went back down the stairs and out the kitchen door. Mrs. Stroud was sitting at the table, shaking her head at life in general.

"What should I do about dinner, tell me that," she called after Mary Lou.

"I'm sure I don't know."

The area behind the house was dominated by a circular

15

driveway which expanded into a graveled car park in front of the former stables, converted now into a three-car garage with an apartment on the second floor for Wayne Stroud. Aunt Eunice's great silver Buick filled the first enclosure; the loss of her license had elevated Wayne to the driver's seat, his joy in manipulating the huge machine not dampened in the least by a steady stream of imprecations from his employer. The garage also housed Uncle Malcolm's black sedan and Uncle Avery's Triumph. Her own dusty little Honda Civic shared the parking area with her parents' modest Ford and Lance's '74 Mustang with the rust-scarred fenders.

Wayne was lovingly polishing the Buick. If he spent half the time on the gardens that he did on the car they could charge admission to the grounds.

"You seen my mother or father?" Mary Lou called, and Wayne jerked a thumb toward the woods. He was in looks much like his mother, of medium height and lean build, dark, taciturn, and bitter, turning over grievances in his mind like the pages of a book. His feelings toward Mary Lou were complex, a combination of derision and a certain reluctant admiration for her indifference to convention. His own goal was the time-worn dream of the poor boy to get rich and show *them,* its attainment rendered improbable given Wayne's lack of industry and imagination, deficiencies vaguely sensed which only served to fuel his anger.

Mary Lou followed a brick path that skirted a small back lawn bordered with day lilies. A second small lawn and garden encircled a sundial in the loop at the top of the circular driveway. Wayne detested both areas, whose dimensions precluded the use of the giant power mower which took second place in his affections only to the Buick. Mary Lou noticed long strands of grass among the lilies, indistinguishable to Aunt Eunice's failing eyesight.

What would happen to Pineacres now? Would Paul want to keep it up? She assumed that it was left to Paul, Aunt Eunice's young adopted son and only child.

The brick path continued beyond the lawn into a wood that extended all the way to Route 117 and made up the larger part of the property. The woods had once been as open as a park and certain areas were still maintained, among them a shadowy pine grove and a stand of beeches, but in the main, the area had reverted to a tangle of second-growth saplings.

In the midst of the circle of beeches, Mary Lou found her mother sitting on a bench in a dilapidated summer house, sedulously working on a watercolor sketch. Mary Lou's mother was an ardent consumer of adult education, having gobbled up courses on Italian cooking, self-defense, personal finance, and palmistry before discovering the arts. Last year's endeavors had filled the house with ceramic ashtrays and misshapen baskets: "Basic Watercolor" had proved a happy choice for the spring and there were pages to go in the catalog.

Two sides of the hexagonal summer house had collapsed completely and the roof was gone. The crumbling edifice in the circle of smooth gray beeches brought to Mary Lou's mind a pagan temple; her mother, bent over her sketchbook in a shaft of sunlight, might just as easily have been preparing for some moonlit rite. She advanced across the clearing, which was carpeted with windflowers, on the cracked and splintered bricks of a path whose condition matched that of its destination.

Ellen Stockbridge raised her head only when Mary Lou's shadow fell across her painting, and she glanced up, vexed, her concentration broken. She liked to feel herself, when in the throes of creativity, lost to the everyday world, risen to a higher plane as it were, and she did not take kindly to thoughtless intrusion by her lumpy, disheveled daughter, who with one glance of utter indifference reduced her work of art to amateur dabbling.

"Well?" she demanded crossly, paintbrush poised.

"Aunt Eunice is dead," said Mary Lou.

"My God, Mary Lou!" cried her mother, leaping to her feet and sending her water cup flying. "You don't sneak up on people with news like that. You lead up to it gently, you damned fool. There are ways to do things and ways not to do things. I suppose I'll have to come back now, won't I," she added in annoyance, bending to retrieve her cup. "Are you sure she's dead?"

"I found her."

"Oh."

"Uncle Malcolm went up, too."

"Oh, all right then. I don't know where your father is."

"He's spying on the Blossoms."

"There you go again. I know where he is and you know where he is but you don't say it out loud. It causes me pain."

Grumpily she gathered up her painting supplies.

"Shall I go find him?"

"No. You can carry these things for me. He'll have to wander in when he's ready. We'll say he's gone for a walk."

Ellen Stockbridge was as short as her daughter and inclined to plumpness but her hair, in contrast to Mary Lou's muddy locks, grew thick and black, only now in her late fifties showing threads of gray. Her wide nose was balanced by a firm chin and the dead-white skin, which lent Mary Lou an appearance of clamminess, provided in her mother a dramatic contrast to her dark hair and eyes.

She wore a white sleeveless blouse imprinted with tiny

18

green acorns and a Kelly green wraparound skirt. Carrying her damp sketch at arm's length, she made her way
gracefully in her canvas espadrilles along the jagged path,
while Mary Lou stumbled behind her bearing sketchbook
and watercolor box. She inevitably grew more awkward
in her mother's presence.

chapter THREE

Uncle Malcolm, Uncle Avery, Aunt Louise, and Lance were sitting stiffly in the living room waiting for Dr. Pearson. All of them, except Avery, had other things to do but it seemed disrespectful to do them. Ellen Stockbridge's arrival caused a welcome diversion and a babble of voices arose.

"Mrs. Stroud is sitting with her."

"She *insisted*."

"Did someone call Paul?"

"Couldn't reach him. He must be on his way."

"Who's going to tell him when he gets here?"

Setting her mother's paint box on the telephone table in the hall, Mary Lou went to stand by the open front door where Lance immediately joined her. The downstairs of Pineacres appeared as gloomy as a mushroom cellar even in the lightest months due to a vast quantity of dark woodwork within and a like profusion of shrubbery without. The winter smell of damp and mold had not yet been completely dissipated but lingered in the atmosphere like a cold reminder of less pleasant things.

"So the old lady's gone," Lance said nervously. "I mean, God, you know I'm sorry she's gone but we can't bring her back, can we? When do you think they'll get to the, you know, the will . . ."

"Ants in your pants?"

"Well, the fact is, I was going to touch her for a bit this

weekend, see. I've got a chance to go to L.A. if I can get a new car."

"I thought you had a backyard full of cannabis."

"Somebody squealed. Can you believe it, Lou, the malice that lurks in the human breast? The cops uprooted every blessed plant and a lot of Mrs. Scanza's marigolds as well."

Lance lived in a room in Somerville where he took advantage of the ingenuousness of his aged landlady. He was definitely not following in his brother's footsteps, having been bounced out of three prep schools and two colleges. Uncle Malcolm was waiting for a prodigal son scene but so far Lance had shown no remorse and was keeping body and soul together satisfactorily with a series of menial jobs. He was currently employed as an elementary school custodian while awaiting his big chance.

"I ask you if this is fair, Lou; I put this to Dad last week, that he give me the money that he would have spent on college since he's not going to spend it, see. So the money is really mine, don't you agree? I mean, jeez, he paid for Bryon to go to college *and* the seminary. Is that fair, Lou?"

". . . all the way out to Chestnut Hill to return her present," announced Ellen Stockbridge's voice from the living room. "I was visiting my dear friend Dorothy Sprague and I saw this nightie, light blue with real Irish lace . . ."

"Oh glory, Ellen," said Louise mournfully, "I got her a nightie, too."

"Well, it doesn't matter now."

"Where the hell is Henry?" Uncle Avery demanded for the third or fourth time.

Dr. Pearson entered through the kitchen door rather than walk around the house to the terrace entrance. He'd taken the time to finish an early supper before making the drive to West Hampford; years of general practice had ingrained in him strength-saving habits. He was a blunt, genial, impatient man, still physically powerful in late middle age, characteristically announcing his arrival with a banging screen door and a shouted hello.

Uncle Malcolm rose to intercept him in the hallway, his own hushed tones rebuking Dr. Pearson's breeziness.

"This is my wife, Louise, Doctor, my brother-in-law, Avery Stockbridge, my sister-in-law, Ellen Stockbridge."

"How do," said Dr. Pearson. "Hi," he shouted to Mary Lou. He recognized that one, although he didn't remember her name; he'd stitched up her lacerated foot when she stepped on a freshwater mussel, the sharp little buggers. Hives another time, or poison oak—she came in with old Mrs. Stockbridge. Odd little thing.

"She upstairs, is she?"

"She's on her bed, Doctor. She was taking a nap," Malcolm murmured unctuously, climbing the stairs behind the physician. His pompous reverence had its usual effect on Mary Lou, who was hard put not to laugh. Not that she cared a bit for Dr. Pearson; when dragged protestingly to his office, his insensitive bellowing humor had closed her up as tightly as the mussel on which she had stepped, but she cheered him on now, as a breath of fresh air. Aunt Louise and Ellen Stockbridge crept demurely up the stairs behind the men, leaving Uncle Avery to dose his shock with his liquid panacea. Her mother, thought Mary Lou, might have been composing herself for a portrait of dignity in grief, but Aunt Louise's freckled Stockbridge face bore signs of agitation, and Mary Lou conceded to her the possibility of genuine distress. She was the least self-centered of the clan, and while she and Graunty had spent much of their time in an undercover battle of wills, that did not preclude affection insofar as Great-Aunt Eunice had been capable of that emotion.

"I suppose we'll have to have a funeral," Lance said gloomily. "What a morbid custom."

"What do you want to do, dig a hole in the backyard?"

"Why not? The Blossoms could dance. And look here, Lou, I could play my guitar and we'd all wear bathing suits and garlands of flowers and Uncle Avery could lay out a table of solace for the mourners."

Mary Lou smiled, glancing through the living room archway at her uncle's semirecumbent form.

"Here comes your pa," Lance said.

Henry Stockbridge was a replica, in a smaller edition, of his sister, Louise, and his cousin, Avery. Thirty years in the United States Army had given him a back as straight as a ramrod. Emerging twelve months previously as a lieutenant-colonel, he kept his shoes shined and his hair short in case he was recalled.

"There's a strange vehicle in the yard, Mary Lou, car with doctor's plates."

"It is a doctor, Dad, Dr. Pearson. He's seeing Great-Aunt Eunice."

"Why is he seeing Aunt Eunice? She was perfectly healthy at lunch. Ate like a horse. Shoulders back, Lance, chin up."

"Come in and have a drink, Henry," Uncle Avery called from the living room. "Come drown your sorrows."

"One minute, Avery, I'm getting briefed. Out with it, Mary Lou. Give it to me straight."

"I'm afraid it's time for taps, Dad."

"Oh my Lord, as bad as that, is it? Left the battlefield, has she? Well, well. Where's your mother?"

"Coming down the stairs with the doctor and Aunt Louise and Uncle Malcolm."

Henry Stockbridge wheeled around and stood at attention at the foot of the stairs so that Dr. Pearson was brought up short on the final step, towering over him like an eagle eyeing a choice morsel.

"My brother-in-law, retired Lieutenant-Colonel Henry Stockbridge," said Malcolm hastily.

"How do, Colonel. Your auntie died in her sleep. The old ticker gave out and she just slipped away."

"An easy death," murmured Henry.

"As you say," Dr. Pearson agreed, moving forward. He winked at Mary Lou in passing and lumbered down the hall; she stared coldly at his back.

"You know who to call now? You have to get the undertaker from Mount Pleasant, Wall and Sons, that's the nearest. They'll transport her to Boston if you decide to have the funeral there."

The voices died away as they passed through the green curtain that hung across the kitchen doorway.

"Paul isn't here yet?" Henry Stockbridge asked his daughter. "He'll have to be told. Do you think I should do it? Heartrending job, informing the next of kin. Malcolm might be a better choice; he has a way with words. I'm just a simple warrior."

"Mary Lou," Louise called out, sweeping back down the hallway with Malcolm in her wake, "could you give Mrs. Stroud a hand? Annie has not shown up."

"You're not thinking of dinner, Louise," Malcolm said in shocked tones, "with Aunt Eunice still in the house?"

"Whether we eat or not will mean nothing to Eunice now," said Louise, "and I do not propose that we all get headaches from hunger, to say nothing of wasting the food. Go along, Mary Lou."

Lance trailed behind her, at loose ends, but Mrs. Stroud shooed him out of the kitchen.

"Go sit with your great-aunt," she told him maliciously, knowing full well it was the last thing Lance would do. "Now that I've been ordered down to cook the dinner, she's left all alone. Not that I expected high-sterical grief, but in the so-called best families someone ought to know the rules of decency. My God, it's a good thing we can't see into the future, isn't it? Only this very afternoon she was standing next to that there table telling me the fish was underdone and now she's made her last complaint. I couldn't believe when I went into that room that she was really gone. I was waiting for her to open them cold gray eyes of hers. 'Mrs. Stroud,' I was waiting for her to say, 'will you kindly not stare at me? Mrs. Stroud, do you think you can follow a simple direction?' Oh, I won't pretend there was no love lost between her and me; she was lady of the manor right from the start. But forty years I've served Eunice Stockbridge, and served is the right word, and forty years lay their mark on a person, and I have to admit, I was just as choked up as if she was my own flesh and blood."

I'll bet you were, thought Mary Lou. I'll bet you took a good rummage through her jewelry case while you had the chance.

Aunt Eunice had ordered vegetable soup, veal par-migian and strawberry shortcake for dinner, and as Mary Lou hulled the strawberries with Mrs. Stroud's bitter comments flowing over and around her own thoughts, she felt tears unexpectedly prick her eyelids at the realiza-tion that her great-aunt would miss the meal. How silly, she told herself scornfully, sniffing back her grief, but Great-Aunt Eunice had been greedy about strawberry shortcake and had waited like a child for the berries to ripen in June. A person complained about the fish at lunch and passed behind the knowledge of shortcake by dinnertime; no wonder they referred to death as the great mystery, thought Mary Lou, and greater minds than mine have grappled with it.

She had hulled and sugared the berries and set the table

by the time Annie shuffled in. Annie took the news lethargically, launching immediately into a lengthy explanation to her mother of the reason for her tardiness, Grandma needing cough syrup and the car wouldn't start and Ray said he would go but first he had to take Junior to work and Junior said . . .

"Listen to me for one minute," Mrs. Stroud said sharply. "There'll be some changes here."

"Should be," said Annie.

Paul arrived at the very moment Mrs. Stroud finished ladling out the vegetable soup and, with unfortunate timing, so did the undertakers, so that Paul rushed into the house in a state of shock. He was supported in his hour of need by the presence of his fiancée, Vangie Pinkham, who was a golden-skinned, golden-haired, self-assured product of years of money and private schooling. She was looking cute as a button in white Calvin Klein jeans and a purple Izod polo shirt. They made, under normal circumstances, a handsome couple. Paul, at twenty-eight, had retained the build of the star athlete which had been his role in prep school and college. He had an open, ingenuous face, untroubled by cares or thoughts and he smiled a lot with straight white teeth. His skin glowed with healthy sunburn, he had thick dark hair and light brown eyes and he was dressed in a white Adidas polo shirt and yellow cotton Levi slacks. He and Vangie rushed into the kitchen hand in hand like something out of a Sunday paper fashion supplement and were immediately engulfed by aunts and uncles with the exception of Uncle Avery, who had drowned his sorrows a bit too deeply and was resting his eyes on the couch in what had once been Uncle Winthrop's den, preserved intact, like a monument to conservative bad taste.

Uncle Malcolm, tugged along by Mary Lou, headed off the undertaker's men in the kitchen and led them up the back stairs. A grumbling Mrs. Stroud returned the vegetable soup to its kettle and Paul was ensconced with a stiff drink in an overstuffed plum-colored velveteen armchair in the living room while his mother was removed with maximum discretion through the kitchen door.

"I just can't believe it," he muttered at predictable intervals, his drink solicitously replenished, or, "Not Mom," or "I just can't grasp it," to which Vangie replied, "It doesn't seem possible," or, "What a terrible shock for you, darling," and Uncle Henry, using the Bokhara rug for a parade ground, instructed him, "Bear up, son, bear up, see it through like a soldier."

Mary Lou wondered if she was the only one getting very hungry and very bored. Perched unobtrusively on a straight chair in the corner of the room, she scrutinized Vangie from the crown of her head to her Bass moccasins, searching for flaws, but gave up, defeated. A pot cover banged in the kitchen; Aunt Louise glanced covertly at her wristwatch.

"I just can't believe it."

"It doesn't seem possible."

Enter Uncle Malcolm with a meaningful look for Aunt Louise that signified the departure of the undertakers with their burden. He settled himself next to the two young people and had just clapped Paul supportively on the knee with a broad hairy hand when Mrs. Stroud dropped what sounded like half the kitchen, there arose such a clatter. Aunt Louise jumped nervously, message received.

"How about a bite to eat, Paul?" she suggested diffidently but with an undercurrent of anxiety.

Paul predictably demurred that he couldn't eat a thing.

Mary Lou could have put the next words in her father's mouth.

"You've got to keep your strength up, Paul. You've got a lot to get through in the next few days."

"You tell him, coach," said Mary Lou. "This is the big one," and there was a fractional stutter in the scene as there so often was after Mary Lou spoke up, as though a smoothly running machine kept hitting a cog slightly out of line.

Without too much persuasion, Paul allowed himself to be led to the table where the reheated soup was put before them at Annie's shuffling pace. His mother's last day was recounted in mournful detail while her veal parmigian disappeared with the speed of melting frost. Lance requested a second shortcake, which was not forthcoming, Mary Lou kicking him sharply under the table just before he said, "Well, where's Graunty's?"

The kitchen having been put to rights, the Strouds departed for an enclave known locally as Dogtown and the Stockbridges gathered in the living room to discuss funeral plans. It was agreed that Aunt Eunice should be buried from the Boston church where she had so long been a communicant; a resting place was assured her next to Uncle Winthrop in the Mount Auburn cemetery. But the date and the time of the services must be decided, the newspapers informed. Malcolm naturally expected to play a part but would he or Aunt Eunice's pastor deliver the eulogy? When a halfhearted wrangle developed between Louise and Ellen as to Aunt Eunice's favorite hymns, Mary Lou wandered into the kitchen for a Coke and a handful of cherries. She found Lance on the back steps moodily swigging a bottle of beer.

"Couldn't lend me five, could you, Lou?" he asked hopefully.

"Nope," said Mary Lou, spitting cherry pits into the darkness. "I'm saving every nickel for a 'Love Boat' cruise."

"Come off it, Lou. I haven't got enough gas to get home."

"Then you'll just have to stay here with the free beer."

"But I don't want to stay here. I mean, there's no point hanging around here now. I can get something out of Ma tomorrow but I kind of hate to barge in there tonight if you know what I mean."

"Your sensitivity is amazing."

By ten o'clock a drift toward bed began to take place; it seemed indecent to go out or to play cards but there was nothing more to be said on the subject of Aunt Eunice or her funeral and the general feeling prevailed that Paul could best be comforted by Vangie. Mary Lou got herself a little bedtime repast from the kitchen, a piece of yesterday's gingerbread and a glass of milk. Lance had disappeared. Probably siphoning gasoline from his father's car. She trudged up the narrow back stairs and was turning on the landing to assault the next and even narrower set to her third-floor bedroom when she was intercepted by her Aunt Louise.

"Mary Lou, would you do something for me, dear. Annie and Mrs. Stroud have left and I forgot to ask one of them to strip Graunty's bed and put the spread on. Somehow it would look less, well, lonely."

She gazed distractedly at the milk and gingerbread. It was a measure of her state of mind that she overlooked their significance, as Mary Lou's tendency to seek comfort in food bespoke a lack of moral fiber repellent to Aunt Louise's steely New England soul, not to mention the squalor of crumbs and dirty glasses in a bedroom.

*   *   *

"So I stripped off the blankets and the sheets," Mary Lou told the two policemen, "and took the case off the top pillow—she always slept with two pillows—and when I picked up the second pillow I noticed reddish smears on the underside and when I looked at the case more closely under a light, I saw that those smears were lipstick and rouge; my great-aunt never appeared in public without makeup, and while she cleaned her face at night, she didn't bother at naptime. That pillow case was clean yesterday morning. I took the sheets out of the linen cupboard to change the bed. So I think," Mary Lou concluded, in a small voice, "that someone must have held that pillow over her face and smothered her."

"For goodness' sake," said Chief Henderson irritably, "that is the last explanation I'd choose. How do you know those stains weren't already on the case? Did you examine every inch of both cases when you made the bed?"

"The pillowcases at Pineacres are ironed; Graunty insisted on it. If there were any stains, Mrs. Stroud or Annie would have seen them while ironing and they would never put a dirty pillowcase in the linen closet. You don't know my great-aunt very well if you think they would."

"So she soiled the case while she was sleeping. Seems easy enough to do. You said the bed covers were all kicked about. Obviously she was restless, rolled around a lot."

"And then woke up," put in Sergeant Putnam helpfully, "and saw that she'd made a mess of the cover, so she shoved that pillow out of sight at the bottom and went back to sleep on a fresh pillow."

"Exactly," said Chief Henderson with satisfaction.

"Not exactly," said Mary Lou. "Graunty wouldn't do that. She wouldn't hide away a mess; she'd expect someone else to clean it up. She would have rung her bell and made Mrs. Stroud climb the stairs and change the pillowcase."

"You can't be sure of that."

"We're wasting time. You'll see what I mean when you look at the pillowcase. It's in my car. I'll go get it."

"Well, okay," Sergeant Putnam agreed when Chief Henderson did nothing but gape at her as though she had made an immoral suggestion. As soon as Mary Lou marched through the doorway, Len exploded.

"Why the hell are you encouraging her, Dave? This is not a psychiatrist's office. She's looking for attention, poor thing, anyone can see that. I don't suppose she gets much. Living with an old lady all summer, changing beds, carrying trays, she sounds like an unpaid servant to me. No wonder she craves a bit of excitement. But it's not fair to play her along."

"It won't do any harm to look at the pillowcase, Len. Then we'll ease her out."

"I guess some people have nothing at all to do this morning," Chief Henderson muttered sourly, but he did, after all, to his surprise, become rather interested in the pillowcase when Mary Lou spread it out upon his desk. Sergeant Putnam pointed out the obvious.

"This mark is the lipstick and here are the two blotches that would correspond to the cheekbones and, look here, Len, at the corners of the mouth there are stiff patches that could be dried saliva."

"Another Shroud of Turin," grumbled Chief Henderson, but he was intrigued despite himself.

"To leave this impression," Sergeant Putnam said, "she would have had to turn over very carefully and press her face straight into the pillow. How likely does that seem?"

"Jeez, Dave, I don't know. I don't know the habits of old ladies. Do they sleep on their faces?"

"C'mon, Len."

"If you're going to ask for an autopsy," Mary Lou suggested, "you'd better call the funeral home pretty soon."

"Autopsy!" snapped Chief Henderson. "Who said anything about an autopsy?"

"It would be a logical next step to look for lint in her lungs."

Sergeant Putnam shook his head in mock admiration. "What else should we do, Miss Stockbridge?"

"Well, I would certainly talk to Dr. Pearson, who signed the death certificate although I doubt if *he* noticed very much. And I'd send that pillowcase to a lab just to make sure it was Aunt Eunice's lipstick and rouge that made the marks. I have samples of both in my purse which I'll leave with you. But I really would get on to the funeral home, if I were you."

chapter FOUR

M ary Lou sat at the kitchen table munching a freshly baked fig square. Although Mrs. Stroud knew very well that the funeral was to take place in Boston, she was unable to control her conditioned response to the fact of death, and cookies were shooting off the baking sheets at a rate that outdistanced even Mary Lou's capacity. Luckily Paul's appetite had not been diminished by his tragedy; neither was Malcolm's intake impaired, although he chewed with an expression of grave detachment as though to stress the insignificance of temporal matters.

Malcolm had appointed himself spokesman for the family and it was he who took the telephone call in mid-morning from Dr. Pearson in which the doctor requested permission for an autopsy on the body of Eunice Stockbridge. Just a couple of little questions here and there, said Dr. Pearson cheerily. Their cooperation, he assured them blandly, might benefit *hundreds* of old people.

Which one of them wished to appear cruelly indifferent to the well-being of the country's senior citizens? Moreover, Paul, whose decision it must ultimately be, seemed to harbor no reservations toward a procedure he regarded as fairly routine. In order to interfere as little as possible with the funeral plans the autopsy could be carried out this very afternoon at the Mount Pleasant Hospital by their most accommodating chief pathologist, Dr. Rupert, who was also, Dr. Pearson neglected to tell the family, the medical examiner for Wessex County.

"Sure, tell him to go ahead. Does he need my signature? I'll be right down. Thanks all the same, cousin Henry, but I think Vangie and I can manage alone."

And Paul set off with an alacrity that might have appeared unseemly if his task were not so somber. His departure gave, as it were, the official seal of approval to the commencement of ordinary activities. Henry, having commended Paul's manly handling of a difficult situation, slipped away behind their backs on another secret reconnaissance mission. Lance departed for Somerville with indecent haste, having wheedled gas money from his mother. Ellen Stockbridge, under the pretense of seeking fresh air, had spent half the morning crouched in the summer house, fooling no one; now, freed from the necessity of guilt, she gathered up her painting supplies, and in Uncle Avery's words, "damn near ran out of the house."

It was left to the remaining three to hammer the issue of autopsy into the ground. There had never been an autopsy in the Stockbridge family and they were divided as to its necessity and propriety. Avery at once suspected gross incompetence or criminal negligence on the part of "that quack country doctor." Louise, on the other hand, interpreted Dr. Pearson's request as a charge of carelessness against the family.

"She took a nap every afternoon," said poor Louise, "every single afternoon. Mary Lou can tell you she always took a nap in the afternoon."

Malcolm comforted her automatically while throwing out a few musing speculations which tended to come too close to the truth for Mary Lou's comfort. She drifted into the kitchen to sample Mrs. Stroud's latest creations and contemplate what she had wrought.

Last evening's horror had carried right through the night and sped her into Hampford this morning. She had acted out of the conviction that someone had done a terrible thing to Great-Aunt Eunice and that someone should be punished. End of Act I: simple, straightforward, and maybe a little bit dumb. The fact that the autopsy was taking place implied that contrary to her expectations, her allegations had not been dismissed as neurotic foolishness, and suddenly the situation took on another dimension, became a little frightening, rather like opening Pandora's box.

Of course, she might be proven wrong. She was wrong so often that this was a consoling thought. How much more pleasant to lay Great-Aunt Eunice to rest without the painful necessity of seeking justice, without the knowledge that the vindication of her suspicions could only be achieved at someone else's expense. Oh damn, thought Mary Lou, reaching for an apple tart. How are the mighty fallen indeed. Great-Aunt Eunice an object on a surgical table when only yesterday she had ruled an empire, however small.

Apparently Mrs. Stroud's mind was running in a similar vein for in between the whirring of mixer blades and the clashing of baking pans, she gave Mary Lou a synopsis of her emotions in the last twenty-four hours, all of which seemed to have found physical manifestation: heartburn, sleeplessness, persistent headache. Thus was Mrs. Stroud's complicated grieving expressed.

A restless night she would certainly grant Mrs. Stroud, thought Mary Lou. She pictured the Stroud tribe huddled around their hearth, Mrs. Stroud, her dark son and daughter, the ancient grandmother—or was it great-grandmother?—and half a dozen other lean brooding Strouds, contemplating their situation. Three jobs Pineacres supplied; Mrs. Stroud lived on her wages the rest of the year. She had kept discreetly silent about the future of the house but surely she must be anxious to know what Paul planned to do. Well, wouldn't Mary Lou like to know, too, just as much as the Strouds? If she inherited a lump sum and Paul sold Pineacres, wouldn't she then be obligated, morally at least, to do something bold and adventurous with her life, relatively speaking, of course. The burden of such a choice was so depressing she thrust it from her mind.

"What I'll always wonder," Mrs. Stroud told her, fanatically greasing yet another tin, "is if she went in her sleep or if she knew what was happening. They say when you're going, your whole life flashes through your mind in a couple of seconds when it's too late to ask forgiveness of certain people."

In the late afternoon, Mary Lou took the canoe for a solitary paddle through the duckweed. Paul and Vangie, entwined in each other's arms, had taken possession of the beach and Mary Lou's presence there would be about as welcome as a maggot's. She stroked conscientiously toward the western shore of the lake, away from the houses and cottages, but the shadowed woods seemed to mock her today with their indifference to human problems. The morning's breeze had dropped and the sun beat up, untempered, from the bronzed surface of the lake. Rubbery water plants gripped her paddle, forcing her to engage periodically in a ridiculous tug-of-war. Moreover, the purpose of the outing was negated by the constant recurrence in her mind's-eye of an image of Great-Aunt Eunice in a giant refrigerator drawer. When letuce and radishes began to share the space, she diagnosed the onset of heat stroke and turned back gratefully toward a vision of a giant ice-cold Pepsi.

Paul and Vangie came out of their own little world long enough to accord her rather surprised recognition.

"My God, Mary Lou," Vangie drawled, "you do think of *the* most hostile ways to enjoy yourself."

Mary Lou gritted her teeth, instantly conscious of rivulets of sweat running from her armpits.

She hauled the canoe onto the sloping deck of the boat house, stood the paddles inside the door, and trudged up the stone steps to the lawn. The Blossoms did not dance on weekends, as they had found themselves the recipients of a certain lack of cordiality on the part of Mrs. Stockbridge's family. A lawn studded with croquet wickets becomes as hazardous as a minefield.

Mary Lou plodded halfway across this sunlit expanse, bathed in the sweet smell of pasture roses, before she raised her eyes to the house. On the terrace sat Uncle Malcolm, Uncle Avery, Aunt Louise, and two familiar policemen.

At the sight of Sergeant Putnam, Mary Lou's heart gave a painful thump.

Oh God, no, she groaned inwardly. A pat on the head and her tongue hung out like Lassie's.

The two men rose to their feet as Mary Lou approached, a courtesy so seldom conceded to Mary Lou that she wondered momentarily who was walking behind her.

*　　*　　*

Sergeant Putnam had, that Saturday afternoon, made one of those compromises indigenous to a policeman's life. He would not go back on his promise of a trip to Mumbo Jumbo, he told his expectant family, but he would have to call Chief Henderson at three o'clock and he might have to cut the outing short. Would they prefer to save the park trip for a full afternoon and see a movie instead? Naturally, there was no consensus. Jenny held out for the lions, Davey mentioned an R-rated film as a possibility, Tom said he didn't care either way to mask the fact that

37

he did, and Barbara wondered what in the world could be happening in Hampford that took precedence over Mumbo Jumbo. In the end they decided on a trip to the video game arcade in Mount Pleasant which seemed sacrilegious on such a bright sunny afternoon, but had the virtue of delivering Sergeant Putnam home by half-past three.

At quarter-past four Chief Henderson called with wonder in his voice.

"There *was* lint in her lungs," he said incredulously. "She *did* die of asphyxiation. The little troll was right. By God, I want to talk to her again. I mean, in how many families when an old person dies, does somebody rush upstairs to check the pillows to see if she was smothered?"

"That's not being fair, Len. She was as surprised as you are."

"Oh, I knew you'd stick up for her. You've got a stray dog complex. You want to watch out that it doesn't interfere with your professional judgment. I've talked to the D.A.'s office. They trust Dr. Rupert implicitly; well, hell, so do I. But it seems so damned unlikely."

Yes, it did, thought Sergeant Putnam. This was not some neglected or isolated old creature falling victim secondarily to vandalism or theft; this was a prominent local citizen, a member of a well-known Boston family, apparently murdered in cold blood on a sunny June afternoon in the midst of a family gathering.

"They want us to proceed with the investigation."

"Hey, that's a feather in your cap."

"Oh, hell, Dave, nobody wants to break up a nice weekend. You can damn well bet that if we come up with anything of interest it will be snatched away on Monday."

"Don't sell yourself short, Len."

"Dave, my stomach is churning like a washing machine. Homicide is out of my league. You know as well as I do that luck played a helluva role in our last two cases."

"So what's the worst that can happen, Len? No gold watch? Plenty of time in the garden? Blue-ribbon cauliflower at the county fair?"

"Blue-ribbon malnutrition," said Len, "if we have to live on my harvests."

chapter FIVE

They left Ted Deegan on duty, cheerfully tapping out an entry on the station's ancient manual typewriter for the *Mount Pleasant Times* "Man in the Kitchen" column.

"Ted's Tasty Turnovers," he announced. "How's that for a creative approach to bananas?"

"It's certainly original," Sergeant Putnam conceded, repressing an urge to gag.

"I think it's going to be even bigger than my broccoli soup," Ted agreed, "which you may recall received the honor of 'Feature of the Week.' "

"In what? the obits?" muttered Chief Henderson, flashing a grin at Sergeant Putnam, but Ted was unperturbed by jocularity. He was twenty years older than Sergeant Putnam and had entered the police department as a patrolman. He would leave with an identical rank, undefiled by any taint of ambition. Like a housewife, Ted filled his days with little treats to break the monotony which was itself a form of security.

With Everett Hewitt on vacation, enjoying a two-week circuit of the best in demolition derbies, the station had lost its overlay of Coke cans and cheese curls bags and pizza crusts and had taken on Ted's tidy touch. The windows sparkled, a jar of coreopsis graced the counter, and the door sprang open to Chief Henderson's hand, on well-oiled hinges.

Sergeant Putnam drove. They proceeded down Main

Street past the bakery and the gift shop and the common, past white picket fences and under heavy-leafed maples and turned west on Route 117, the Mount Pleasant–Fordham road, following its undulating surface beyond the elementary school and Scanlon's truck farm, past the housing developments of Spruce Ridge and Apple Valley where ten-year-old Capes were losing shingles and shutters, where doors warped and windows jammed.

Chief Henderson, clutching his notebook like a good-luck charm, sucked on a Lifesaver and allowed himself to be momentarily distracted by the passing scene.

Arthur Sheppard's farm, empty since the death of the town's filthiest recluse, gazed at them mournfully through broken windows from a yard full of weeds.

"Little buggers have been busy," commented Chief Henderson, eyeing the jagged panes. "Be a shame if they set the place on fire someday."

"The sooner the better," agreed Sergeant Putnam, remembering with a shudder the sights and smells of Arthur's kitchen, as dark and fetid as an animal's lair.

"Rocky Meadows is empty again."

The farm's battered blue mailbox hung forlorn and askew at the end of the driveway.

"Those kids didn't make a go of it, either. I was glad that Mrs. Atkins unloaded the place though."

"Marginal farming, Dave," Chief Henderson told him, "has become a luxury. All these fields will soon be woods. We're going back to the forest."

As if to confirm his opinion, they drove for several miles through second-growth timber where the trees resembled an army of unhealthy recruits, spindly and crooked, and the damp forest floor sprouted fountains of ferns. Here and there someone had hacked out a clearing like his pioneer ancestors and raised a split level or a ranch house on a patch of raw soil. The settlement of

West Hampford flashed past; a white church at a cross-roads, a general store behind gas pumps, a handful of houses, an orchard neatly walled, then, insidiously, the woods crept in again.

"What the hell's that?"

Beside a rustic log cabin, the Blossoms of God swarmed over a vegetable garden, hoeing, weeding, and chanting. Chief Henderson turned around to stare at them.

"Is that where they live? Whatever they are?"

"Blossoms of God, Len."

"Can't they be religious in jeans? Turn left up ahead, Dave, where it says private road. We're almost there," he added nervously. "You know I think I've been up here maybe two or three times in all these years. These aren't the kind of people who need cops. There's a lot of old money up here, Dave."

"This is not a social call. You are an experienced police officer investigating a probable case of homicide. That's all you have to remember."

"And that's supposed to comfort me, knowing *I'm* in charge?"

About a quarter of a mile down a well-graded dirt road they reached on their left two stone pillars as massively misproportioned as the house behind them and bearing between them a wooden arch on which had been immodestly engraved with great whacks of an ax:

PINEACRES

C. W. STOCKBRIDGE

"Eunice's husband was Winthrop," said Chief Henderson, "and Winthrop's father was Henry. Who the hell is C.W.?"

The driveway wound between grass verges backed by

massed rhododendrons and as they neared the house, a skillful planting of specimen trees: flowering crabs and cherries. Sparrows were fluttering and splashing in a birdbath set amid a circle of heavy-headed peonies. Both men recognized immediately, in the first bay of the garage, Eunice Stockbridge's infamous Buick. A lean dark man dressed in jeans and a grease-stained gray tank top was applying metal polish to the front bumper.

He straightened up and gazed insolently at the cruiser, resting one hip against a fender; Chief Henderson retaliated by ignoring him completely and marching briskly toward the back door, which was opened in answer to his knock by a middle-aged woman who bore a marked familial resemblance to the bumper polisher, even to the same cold disdain. But Chief Henderson was not deterred by a little hostility. Gone now was all hesitation; all signs of insecurity had dropped away like a cloak at the moment of confrontation. He insinuated himself deftly into the kitchen even as he asked for Paul Stockbridge.

"Well, I don't know where Paul is, I'm sure," said Mrs. Stroud unhelpfully, momentarily forced to give ground. "I'm a cook not a nursemaid."

As she continued to remain rooted to her personal square of linoleum, Chief Henderson suggested that someone else might know where Paul could be found, if there was anyone else at home.

"They're all here," Mrs. Stroud replied. "You want to talk to one of them, do you, instead of Paul?"

"I would like to talk to Paul, if Paul can be found," Chief Henderson explained with admirable forbearance. "If not, perhaps one of them can tell me where he *can* be found."

"Maybe, maybe not."

Crossing the kitchen, Mrs. Stroud pulled back the green curtain that hung in the doorway, and sticking her head beyond its heavy folds, shouted, "Mr. Malcolm, there's cops in the kitchen."

"Might as well say dogs on the doorstep," Chief Henderson muttered to Sergeant Putnam, who was admiring his well-appointed surroundings. The room was redolent of the scents of spices, vanilla, and chocolate and his mouth began to water. Mrs. Stroud had disappeared momentarily behind the curtain in answer to an unintelligible query; now she bobbed into sight again.

"This way," she ordered them curtly. "Mr. Malcolm is on the terrace."

The faintly Victorian air of this pronouncement served as an appropriate transition from the modern world of the kitchen to the dim, overstuffed precincts beyond. The hall was as cavernous as a subway tunnel and they threaded their way toward distant light through a forest of immovable objects, including a receptacle stuffed with canes and rolled umbrellas that Sergeant Putnam wonderingly identified as the lower half of an elephant's leg.

Mrs. Stroud held open the screen door, shooed them through summarily and deserted them on a sunny terrace of local fieldstone which was furnished with an eclectic collection of wrought iron and wicker, the majority of the chairs and their inhabitants huddled around a central table above which rose a striped sun umbrella. The terrace was edged with a low stone wall on which were massed pots of geraniums, their candy colors shining brightly against a backdrop of lush green lawn. Several larger redwood planters contained fig and citrus trees.

Chief Henderson paused to accord the scene a gardener's appraisal, awarded it the Leonard Henderson nod of approval, and turned to the human element in the landscape.

Rising to his feet was a stout hairy man in a cream-colored polo shirt and madras Bermuda shorts, behind whom sat two archetypical Yankees, the trio immediately cast frivolously by Sergeant Putnam and quite despite himself as the characters in an imaginary children's book: Charley Chimp and his Ferret Friends.

He kicked himself mentally for his disrespect when Charley introduced himself as Reverend Malcolm Turnbull.

Why, the fellow carries his own hair shirt, thought Sergeant Putnam, which necessitated another kick.

The three on the terrace, for their part, saw before them the arm of the law, somewhat more impressive in form than might have been expected in a town the size and rusticity of Hampford. For Chief Henderson drew stature from his position and when representing the forces of righteousness, he assumed a posture so straight and an expression so stern that he might have passed for an Old Testament prophet. Sergeant Putnam proved reassuring through sheer bulk. He had the reliable solidity of a rock and projected a boyish ingenuousness with his freckled face and candid blue eyes. Both men were dressed in navy blue trousers and jackets, sky-blue shirts, and navy ties.

Chief Henderson explained that he was looking for Paul Stockbridge.

"Yes, indeed, so Mrs. Stroud said. Been going a little fast in that expensive toy of his, ha ha?"

"The matter concerns his mother, the late Eunice Stockbridge," said Chief Henderson gravely, disdaining levity. "May I offer my condolences on her passing?"

"But that's just where Paul has gone," put in one of the seated figures eagerly, a middle-aged woman who, unlike the other two, was situated in the full sun, her hands tightly clasped.

"My wife, Louise," Reverend Turnbull interjected hastily. "Her cousin, Avery Stockbridge."

45

Avery, who had been reclining on a chaise longue with a drink in his hand, swung his feet to the terrace and his face emerged from shadow with the sharp bright edge of a hatchet.

"Paul has gone into town on business concerning his mother," Louise Turnbull told the policemen.

"Are you referring to the autopsy?"

"So that's common knowledge, is it?" she retorted bitterly. "I simply cannot understand the purpose behind this indignity."

"My wife was very close to her dear auntie," explained Malcolm Turnbull solicitously. "She is distraught; we are all distraught; I shall not make excuses for our state of mind. Death is upsetting," he announced heavily as though stating a profundity worth transcribing. "The passage of our nearest and dearest is distressing enough without the addition of what my wife has so rightly termed 'this indignity.' I beg to disagree, however, dear, with your statement about Paul. Paul has returned from town. I have seen him."

"Well, I haven't."

"I'll go look for him, shall I?" Avery volunteered, taking up his empty glass and recalling his cousin to a habit of hospitality which on normal occasions must have been second nature to her, but which was, today, mechanical.

"Would you like a glass of iced tea, gentlemen? Won't you please sit down while Avery is looking for Paul."

They sat, side by side on two white Italian wire chairs with yellow cushions. Malcolm Turnbull also sat.

"I don't suppose," he murmured, leaning forward conspiratorially, "I don't suppose you'd like to fill us in a bit on the purpose of this visit? We're all cousins, you know, even though Paul is so much younger, all united in our affection for Aunt Eunice and in our concern that nothing mar the decorum of her final rites."

Chief Henderson appeared to consider this appeal while studying a particular geranium of an almost lavender hue that he would like to see in his own garden. He was saved from the necessity of an answer by the appearance at the end of the lawn of a familiar toadlike figure.

Mary Lou was dressed in a pair of shorts which Barbara Putnam would have termed god-awful, constructed of some kind of sleazy stretch material that was stretched just about to its limit, paired with a white T-shirt with red lettering that caused Sergeant Putnam to sit up and blink, for he could swear that spun across her heavy bosom was the label *Mentally Retarded.* She was quite a bit closer before he made out the rest of the slogan, in smaller letters above the logo: *1983 Walk for the . . .* Mary Lou tripped on the terrace steps and raised a red damp face to the gathering.

"Mary Lou," Mrs. Turnbull called anxiously, with no attempt at introductions, "these policemen want to talk to Paul and we don't know where he is."

"He's down on the beach with Vangie," answered Mary Lou indifferently, and to Sergeant Putnam's amazement, Mrs. Turnbull blushed darkly. Did she find it reprehensible that Paul was lounging on the beach with a girlfriend twenty-four hours after his mother's death or did she fear that they would find it so?

"Vangie is Paul's fiancée," Louise Turnbull explained, as though this fact made the situation more decorous. "Mary Lou, please go down and tell him to come up here at once."

Mary Lou turned without a word and plodded back the way she had come. Sergeant Putnam caught a sly glance from Chief Henderson. Well, they *did* treat her abominably, but no protest would cross *his* lips. They sat and watched Mary Lou's progress across the lawn. The atmosphere had grown turgid with tension, which did not in itself, alas, constitute evidence of foreknowledge, as it might as easily be a general familial anxiety in the face of a real or imagined threat to the status quo. Louise worked her hands together; Malcolm had fallen into a heavy-browed silence. Chief Henderson took advantage of the lull to ask pleasantly for the name of the lavender geranium.

chapter SIX

Within a few minutes, Mary Lou had reversed direction, and like a wind-up toy, was moving back toward the terrace in the same dogged shuffle while on her heels tripped a young Greek god, muscles gently aripple, accompanied by his consort, who glistened as though varnished with suntan oil. Paul, who was wearing nothing but swimming trunks, stepped gracefully onto the terrace, acknowledged the two policemen with a polished prep school handshake, and swung lazily onto a chaise beside his cousin's chair.

"More botheration?" he asked genially, waving off Vangie, who murmured something about getting dressed. She crossed paths with Avery Stockbridge as he emerged from the house with a fresh drink in his hand.

"Huzza, I've found him," Avery announced, seeing Paul established on flowered cushions, and stumbling a bit, due to the unevenness of the stone surface, he made a precarious return to his own chaise while Mary Lou slumped on the terrace wall, shoulder to leaf with a potted geranium.

"Now, what's this all about?" Paul smiled with a dazzle of white, exuding ease and charm. His dark-lashed ginger-brown eyes were startlingly clear and attractive against the warmer tone of his skin. And what a lot of that warm brown skin was exposed to admiration! Sergeant Putnam noted with petty satisfaction that his chest was as smooth as a girl's.

"We had a visit this morning," Chief Henderson said, plunging right in, "from Miss Mary Lou Stockbridge. While stripping her great-aunt's bed yesterday evening, she noticed certain inconsistencies which worried her very much, so much so that she felt impelled to tell someone about them."

"But not her family," said Malcolm bitterly. Here then was the betrayal; Mary Lou had gone over their heads, had risen out of her place, had opened the door marked private to God knows what or who. Four heads turned as one, four hostile gazes fell on Mary Lou, who returned their attention defiantly. Paradoxically, the degree of tension both rose and fell. Sergeant Putnam could almost hear the unspoken words, What has she done now?, expressed with a kind of dread, and at the same time a lessening of that dread with the contradictory unvoiced thought that if Mary Lou had done something, it could only be, by definition, insignificant.

Was it his imagination or did Chief Henderson derive a certain malicious pleasure from informing Paul Stockbridge, "The autopsy that was performed on your mother has corroborated certain points that were raised by your niece. Eunice Stockbridge died of asphyxiation and on the basis of traces of pillow lint in her throat and lungs, her death is being regarded as inflicted by an outside party; to put it bluntly, Mrs. Stockbridge was smothered to death."

"Good God," cried Paul, gazing about him wildly with outstretched arms as though seeking Vangie's solace.

While Mary Lou remained impassive by her geranium, Sergeant Putnam studied the remaining faces. Avery Stockbridge, slopping his drink, jolted upright with an expression less shocked than amazed. Malcolm looked horrified, as well he might, and Louise Turnbull blanched until her freckles stood out like Grape-Nuts.

Then Avery laughed. "Come off it," he stuttered, focusing on Chief Henderson. "You . . . you are not honestly going to sit there and t-tell me that you were taken in by our little Mary Lou? You have to watch this little old niece of mine," he added, wagging a finger playfully at a grim-faced Mary Lou. "She's got a fertile imagination and a lot of time on her hands. Do you think if I had stripped my aunt's bed or Louise had done it or Malcolm, that we would have come running to you with a tale of murder and mayhem?"

"I doubt it very much," said Chief Henderson dryly.

"This business of lint in the lungs," Avery scoffed. "We're living in a dusty old house."

"Those heavy cotton sheets are *very* linty," Louise added eagerly.

"The hell with the lint!" Paul interrupted harshly, sitting forward. "I want to know about these inconsistencies noted by my bright-eyed niece. Where are the facts? You could be sued for busting in here making this kind of accusation unless you've got some goddamn good reasons."

"When Miss Stockbridge removed the pillows from your mother's bed last night, she noticed marks of cosmetics on the underside of the bottom pillow. The state police lab has confirmed that the marks on the case were made by the cosmetics furnished by Miss Stockbridge from your mother's supply: Hawaiian Sunset rouge and Fire Hydrant lipstick. Are you familiar with these cosmetics, Mrs. Turnbull?"

"Yes, I am," Louise admitted. "My aunt used the same unfortunate color combination for years. I've bought both for her from time to time."

"Thank you. Now, in order to leave these particular marks on the case, Mr. Stockbridge, your mother would have had to press the pillow onto her face or press her face straight into the pillow; neither course of action seems likely."

"That's it?" Paul asked incredulously. "That's all the evidence you have? She might have fallen on her face when her heart gave out."

"She was found on her back, Mr. Stockbridge, a position she did not assume after death, nor is it likely in the same condition that she removed the top pillow. Furthermore, her heart did not give out. She was in excellent health for a woman of her age. Now, I don't want to argue with you folks and I don't intend to. I'm here in cooperation with the district attorney's office to commence an investigation into the death of Eunice Stockbridge and that's what I'm going to do. In addition to asking a few questions, I must seal your aunt's room before I leave today and those seals are not to be broken until the arrival of the state police lab crew. I personally do not interpret these actions as threatening, but you are of course welcome to engage legal counsel."

"We certainly shall," Malcolm said decisively. "I will make the call at once. I do find these actions threatening, sir, insinuating and threatening, and I intend to clear up the matter with alacrity. Our family is not without certain connections."

"What about the funeral?" ventured Louise.

"It may be delayed. There will be an inquest."

"Oh, wonderful," Paul cried, jumping to his feet. "Mal, go make your call. Let's put an end to this farce."

Vangie chose this moment to make her entrance, poised and perfect in a stunning yellow sundress; she held her pose valiantly as the moments ticked by, but Paul's gaze remained focused gloweringly on the two policemen, while the rest of the family directed its attention to the confrontation.

"Why don't you sit down, Vangie?" asked Mary Lou

sweetly. Vangie, outmaneuvered, shifted to the offensive and ran to take a stand beside Paul.

"Whatever's the matter, darling?"

"Just a minute, dearest," Paul ground out, staring bitterly at Chief Henderson, who stared back blandly.

"I shall need a statement from each of you concerning your actions yesterday afternoon."

"I don't believe this," Paul cried. "It's like a scene from a third-rate play."

"You won't get one word from us until we have legal representation," snapped Malcolm Turnbull.

"You have the right to counsel," Chief Henderson agreed.

"I don't know why we shouldn't tell him where we were," said Louise. "I have nothing to hide."

"None of us has anything to hide, Louise. That's not the point."

"Well, I think he ought to know about those Blossoms of God roaming all over the place."

The effect of this statement was electric. Glances jumped from one to the next, met and meshed. The escape hatch had just been opened. Was Louise Turnbull really that clever, wondered Sergeant Putnam, or was she guileless?

"Blossoms of God have been over here?" asked Chief Henderson.

"It's a religious group, what I guess you'd call a cult," Louise explained. "They live down on the main road and somehow or other my aunt came into contact with them and they became quite friendly in the sense that they were up here at all hours, dancing and prancing on the lawn. She claimed they amused her but we have seriously considered whether they had somehow brainwashed her. I mean it. Why else would she allow such liberties? Yesterday I saw one going down the stairs from the second-floor landing and that's not the first time I've seen one in the house."

"Could you be a little more specific, Mrs. Turnbull? At what time did you see this Blossom?"

"About half-past four."

"And what were you doing at that time?"

"Are you doubting my word?"

"I'm just trying to visualize the scene."

"I see. Well, I came upstairs at four intending to take a short rest in my room but I was sidetracked with this and that and it must have been at least four-thirty when I came out into the hall and saw him. I was in my room for some time after that before I heard Mary Lou come upstairs and she came at five, so I think I can safely place the incident about half-past four."

"How were you sidetracked?"

Louise said icily, "I was sewing some buttons on my son's shirt. I passed the door to his room on the way to my own and noticed that some of his clothes were strewn across the floor. There were two buttons off his shirt. I went across the hall to the sewing room and there I put on new buttons. Coming out of the sewing room, I saw a yellow-robed figure going down the front stairs."

"Thank you, Mrs. Turnbull."

"If I thought one of them had actually . . . my God," said Paul. "But why?"

"Could it have been part of some hideous ritual?" Malcolm asked with a shudder. "You read about such things happening, but that poor Eunice should have gotten mixed up with something like this hardly bears contemplation. Well," he said, rousing himself, "I'm going to call Alden, Alden and Standish and see what they suggest we do."

"Then I'll affix the seals. Perhaps you would be kind enough to show us the way, Mrs. Turnbull?"

Before Louise could reply, the screen door banged open and Mrs. Stroud appeared within its frame with the dramatic abruptness of a psychic illusion.

"Dinner is served," she bawled flatly.

"Oh my goodness," said Louise. "I specifically requested an early meal. Oh gracious, we can't keep her waiting; she would be mortally offended."

"Then let's eat," said Avery. "Mary Lou can take the cops upstairs. Where the hell are your parents anyway, Mary Lou? They never seem to be around when they should be."

"They can't expect to have hot meals," agreed Louise crossly, "if they can't get here on time."

Nobody appeared to be at all concerned about the temperature of Mary Lou's dinner. A general shuffle took place toward the door, Mary Lou plodding along at the end of the line. In the murk of the hallway they came upon Henry Stockbridge replacing a walking stick in the elephant's leg.

"Chow time," he said cheerfully.

"Where have you been?" Louise asked with some asperity. "Didn't you hear us out there? You should have been with us, Henry."

"Give me five reasons why," Henry answered, springing forward to shake hands with the two policemen. "Thirty years of active service," he explained. "I have to be on the go. Don't let me hold you up; you're men of action, too. Louise will brief me."

And with these words he spun about-face and marched toward the dining room into which Paul and Vangie had already disappeared. The others now straggled after them except for Malcolm, who was dialing a number on the hall telephone. Without a word, Mary Lou began to climb the stairs and the policemen followed her pale fat legs which gleamed dimly before them like phosphorescent sausages.

"Where is Mrs. Turnbull's room?" Chief Henderson asked when they stood in the long narrow hallway at the top of the stairs.

"The second door on the left."

"And your cousin's?"

"The last room on the right."

"So how did your aunt pass your cousin's room and notice his clothes on the floor? Is there another stairway at the back of the house?"

"She didn't have to pass his room," said Mary Lou. "She could have come up the front stairs and scurried down the hall like a busy little chipmunk for the sole purpose of pawing through his things. She knew he was down at the shore."

"Why would she do that?" Sergeant Putnam wondered.

"Because she wanted to find out what he's up to. Lance makes his parents very nervous."

"So you don't think she was sewing on buttons in the sewing room?"

"Oh yes, I think that part is true, that she found his clothes thrown all over the place and was disgusted because that kind of slackness is morally repugnant to Aunt Louise."

"The important point," Chief Henderson broke in impatiently, "as far as her story is concerned, is not *why* she went into her son's room but whether or not she *was* in that room or the sewing room at the back of the house, at the other end of the corridor from her aunt's room, for approximately half an hour, between roughly four and four-thirty."

"The important point is telling the truth," said Mary Lou. "But I don't suppose you get much of that in your profession."

Sergeant Putnam bit his lip at the expression on Len's face.

"I don't think we need keep you any longer, Miss Stockbridge," Chief Henderson said stiffly.

"Don't you think you ought to hear about the man who's been hanging around the grounds?"

Chief Henderson, who had turned toward Eunice Stockbridge's bedroom door, turned back toward Mary Lou.

"What man?" he asked suspiciously.

"Well, *I* don't know what man. That's for you to find out. I've seen him twice, once at the edge of the woods and once behind the garage. He's middle-aged, I'd say, kind of heavy and baldish and he was wearing jeans and a white T-shirt. I'd like to tell you that he had a scar on his chin or a mole on his nose or six fingers on one hand but I was too far away for a good look."

"This man behind the garage," Chief Henderson repeated with palpable disbelief. "Has anyone else seen him?"

"I mentioned him to my cousin Lance yesterday afternoon while we were lying on the beach. He took it about as seriously as I expected he would."

"Hmmm, yes, I see. Thank you, Miss Stockbridge," said Chief Henderson. He gripped the metal rod behind the doorknob and turning it, opened the door.

"Do you know if anyone's been in here since last night? Anyone come in to clean or tidy the room?"

"I don't know if anyone's been in here or not," said Mary Lou, "because I am not omniscient. But no one has cleaned or tidied. The bedding is right where I left it."

She looked around the room carefully. It seemed exactly as she had last seen it except that Aunt Eunice's teeth had gone with her.

The two men made a slow circuit of the bedchamber,

studying its contents thoughtfully while Mary Lou stood in the middle of the space, keeping her fingerprints off flat surfaces. Chief Henderson peered out an open front window, noting a straight drop to the terrace below; side windows overlooked the gently sloping roof of an addition which Mary Lou identified as the sunroom.

"Any windows open here yesterday afternoon, Miss Stockbridge?"

"The same two that are open today."

"When you came up with the tray yesterday afternoon was the bathroom door closed?"

"It was always closed. Aunt Eunice was not the kind of person who wanders around with a toilet staring her in the face."

With Mary Lou breathing moistly at his elbow, Chief Henderson put in place the seals that would render the room inviolate until its next group of official visitors. Once again they threaded their way down the twilit staircase.

"I'd like one last word with your Uncle Malcolm if you'd be kind enough to fetch him. I'd rather not disturb the meal."

"Gracious no," agreed Mary Lou. "Let them plan my lynching undisturbed."

She plodded in the direction of the dining room, leaving Sergeant Putnam grinning by the elephant's leg.

"I don't see what's so goddamn funny," grumbled Chief Henderson, whose own three daughters were satisfyingly ordinary in thought, word, and deed. "I think she's pathetic. Why are we standing in this mausoleum? Let's go into the kitchen."

Wayne Stroud and his mother were seated at the table, Wayne confronting a heaping plate of New England boiled dinner that made Sergeant Putnam go weak in the knees, while Mrs. Stroud mopped gravy from her plate with a biscuit that ought to be immortalized. They exhibited identical expressions of irritability at the intrusion.

"Not everyone could be a policeman," Mrs. Stroud observed, "bursting into houses of mourning, riding roughshod over the innermost feelings of decent people."

"We're on our way," Chief Henderson told her cheerfully. "This your son, Mrs. Stroud?"

"This is Wayne," Mrs. Stroud admitted reluctantly.

"Fine-looking boy," Chief Henderson needled him, while Wayne assaulted his meat as though it were Chief Henderson's hide.

"Well, well, here you are," cried Malcolm Turnbull affably, striding into the room with his napkin in his hand. "I was fortunate to reach Charles Alden himself at home, Chief Henderson, before he left for a dinner party. He'll make a few strategic phone calls tonight on our behalf and will be out here tomorrow morning to give us the benefit of his expertise."

"That's fine, Mr. Turnbull. I'll be out here, too."

Mrs. Stroud snorted at this prospect but Malcolm was in buoyant spirits now that he had the promise of a little high-quality legal assistance to reduce this ridiculous allegation to its proper proportions.

He ushered the two men toward the door which swung open even as he reached for it, admitting Ellen Stockbridge, draped with painting supplies and bearing yet another damp achievement.

"What's happened?" she demanded, staring at the policemen, who stared back.

"My sister-in-law," Malcolm muttered. "Mrs. Henry Stockbridge."

This was Mary Lou's mother? This striking woman with her gleaming black hair and clear white skin? What kind of a relationship could they have, she and her

59

daughter? Or she and her husband for that matter, old Active Harry.

"What's the matter?" Ellen asked more sharply.

"If you had been here this afternoon, I would not have to go through the whole story again, Ellen," Malcolm told her with more than a trace of irritation. "I'll explain at the table where I left my meal congealing on its plate."

"And boiled dinner your very favorite," cried Mrs. Stroud in sympathy. "Police brutality wears many cloaks."

"For goodness' sake, Mrs. Stroud, that's enough," said Ellen crossly and Malcolm, with some embarrassment, bade his visitors good night.

chapter SEVEN

Sergeant Putnam dreamed of fire alarms and struggled to consciousness sniffing the air for smoke. The telephone on the bedside table was ringing into his ear and he reached for it groggily. A change had taken place in the weather overnight; the sky was heavily overcast and the dim light which filtered through the drawn curtains enhanced his impression of having been aroused from a predawn stupor. The hands of the alarm clock, however, stood at quarter of eight, and the murmur of a television set from the living room downstairs proved that at least one of the children was already up, dribbling milk and Sugar Corn Pops on the couch.

Barbara muttered something unintelligible as Sergeant Putnam lifted the receiver and Len's cheery greeting assailed him. Len was afflicted with the inability to sleep after four o'clock in the morning, a condition that had crept up on him insidiously with advancing age and was accompanied by a nauseous self-righteousness, so that he was not only as bright as a robin in the early hours but scornful of those who had not mowed a lawn or felled a tree by seven o'clock.

"Hey, Dave," he said, assuming, despite continuous evidence to the contrary, that Sergeant Putnam was also in the middle of his day, "they were right about connections. Boy, were they right. I've never seen things take off so fast. You know who's on the way out to Pineacres right now, at eight o'clock on a Sunday morning? The lab boys, that's who. The inquest is scheduled for Tuesday and you and I are going to be 'cooperating' henceforth not only with our old pal Walfield but with an assistant D.A. called Lowell. Walfield I might expect, but a Lowell?"

"Out and out intimidation."

Lieut. Edward Walfield of the Massachusetts State Police was Chief Henderson's personal cross. While state and local services maintained a unified facade against the forces of evil, deep crosscurrents churned beneath the surface. Chief Henderson's attitude was typical of small-town policemen. While readily admitting to doubts as to his competency to handle the "big ones," he turned prickly as a cactus at the intrusion upon his territory by more experienced law officers, and scathingly regarded Walfield's successes as totally dependent upon the laboratory facilities and electronic communications systems which were provided for his use. There was nothing Chief Henderson liked better than to score a point for old-fashioned sleuthing, even while grudgingly admiring and freely employing those same facilities whose use by Lieutenant Walfield he considered effeminate. It was all very complicated.

"I'm not abdicating this case without a helluva shove," he told Sergeant Putnam, into the very same ear to which he had the day before expounded his inadequacies. "We're going to be right there at ten o'clock with the Aldens and the Lowells and the Stockbridges. I'll swing by and pick you up about nine-thirty."

"Right, Len. I'll be ready."

"Cock-a-doodle-doo," murmured Barbara, opening her eyes. "That could only be our early bird. What's he dreamed up now?"

"Looks like an interesting day."

"For whom? The kids and me? No, I shouldn't say that. I'm as shocked as you are. It's a funny thing," she said, sitting up and looking as fresh as did many of her contemporaries after an hour with cosmetics, "but I don't like to hear about old ladies smothered with pillows. I hope you catch who did it real quick. Do you really think it could be one of *them?*"

Sergeant Putnam levered himself from a prone position and swung his feet onto the floor.

"Damn," he said, "I guess I might as well get up."

"You said they were hostile yesterday, the family, I mean."

"Angry. Angry at being put on the spot. Angry with Mary Lou for putting them on it."

"They'd rather she hadn't said anything?"

"Sure. It's as though there's only a murder because she called attention to it."

"Well, good for her," said Barbara stoutly. "You stick up for Mary Lou, Dave; I think she's going to need a friend. Now," she said, pulling on her bathrobe, "if you're going out to get justice done, I'm going to cook you a breakfast that will give you the strength of Superman. How about eggs and hash browns?"

"And sausages?" asked Sergeant Putnam hopefully.

*   *   *

The confrontation took place in the living room at Pineacres due to weather conditions which had worsened by ten o'clock. Light rain was falling intermittently as though from a giant sprinkling can. The cushioned chairs on the terrace wore transparent tents of plastic and the flagstones glistened darkly. The lake mirrored the sullen gray of the sky.

Dampness had permeated the house as well and the

hallway seemed particularly dank and cheerless even though several lights were on. Lieutenant Walfield, who had come out with the lab team, greeted Chief Henderson and Sergeant Putnam outside the living room door with just the slightest hint of condescension. He was looking his immaculate best in tailored tunic and trousers and shiny boots and Sergeant Putnam fought back an urge to surreptitiously wipe the toes of his own scuffed oxfords on the back of his wrinkled pants. Once Walfield entered the living room, however, he was just another cop. The caste lines were clearly drawn. A coffee service and a plate of sweet rolls on a table beneath the windows bespoke the presence of Mrs. Stroud, although the two Hampford men had not encountered her, having come through the front door in an attempt to lend as much dignity as possible to their arrival.

Malcolm Turnbull, they were soon to learn, had risen at the crack of dawn to reach his suburban St. Cuthbert's, conduct the early service and return to Pineacres by midmorning. Lance had been summoned back from Somerville. It was the family's consensus that he was best kept under its collective thumb.

Charles Alden held a cup and saucer in the center of a little group consisting of Avery, Paul, and Vangie. His summer suit, casually mussed, was meticulously tailored to his lanky form and slight stoop; he wore an Eliot House tie. His gray hair swept back along his bony skull to a fringe at the collar, he had a jutting nose and sharp blue eyes, the overall effect being of some long-legged wading bird.

Paul and Avery were drinking what looked like orange juice, although judging from Avery's degree of animation, the juice was orange in color only. Louise stood a little apart with young George Lowell, discussing Race Week in Marblehead. Mr. Lowell was misrepresented by his name; in those initial few seconds of blank regard when one is passed or failed, Mr. Lowell had been found lacking in the ever so subtle requirements for inclusion. There was a slight beefiness that suggested a little Kozlowski or Vogelsanger; surely a little O'Malley in that black hair and those thick lashes. The suit, although identical in cut and material to Mr. Alden's, was nevertheless a little stiff, the shoes a little too new. Within the space of a handshake, he had been rejected as genuine Lowell, this knowledge in the same instant imparted to him, as it was meant to be, always graciously, never a scene, but the judgment having been made there was no appeal. His laughter was just a little strained. Louise played the hostess impeccably.

The Henry Stockbridge family were lined up glumly on the couch as though they had been told to sit still and keep quiet while the rest of the clan repaired the damage. Henry's toes were tapping, his body mired in unnatural inactivity, Ellen looked both bored and resentful, and Mary Lou was contemplating the bulges of her midsection which were encased in rolls of pink cotton T-shirt with which she was wearing a bedraggled denim skirt and black ballerina slippers. As the policemen's legs moved into her line of vision she looked up and said, "Hi." It was the only greeting they received.

When Mr. Alden had finished his coffee and his conversation, Louise called Henry into action, rather fussily bidding him to drag chairs and push back tables, ensuring that all the principals were seated. Lieutenant Walfield ignored the straight chair on the periphery of the gathering which was indicated as his, taking instead an armchair directly across from Mr. Alden. Chief Henderson and Sergeant Putnam fared less well and were stranded in suburbia.

George Lowell commenced proceedings with a deferential speech in which he seemed to be begging pardon on behalf of the district attorney's office for even considering this a case of homicide and heaven forbid that any one of them should come under suspicion. Lieutenant Walfield sat impassively through these preliminaries, then announced flatly, "I'll see each one of you alone in the presence of Mr. Alden. I'll start with Mrs. Turnbull. The rest of you will wait in the next room to be called."

The effect of this announcement on the gathering was most unsettling. This was not a family used to finding itself part of an impersonal system. For the first time they seemed to comprehend that they were enmeshed in a situation that was beyond their control. All the connections in the world were not going to abridge, modify, or delete the word murder. Aunt Eunice's death was not a product of Mary Lou's fevered imagination, it was not due to a clerical error or a bungled autopsy; Aunt Eunice had been smothered with a pillow, and as a result of that action, this beady-eyed, ill-mannered individual had the right to invade their home and badger them with impudent questions.

Anger and fear were the products of this growing sense of helplessness, but if Lieutenant Walfield found himself suddenly ringed by a circle of both, he maintained his imperturbability. Lieutenant Walfield was not a humanist. He ground remorselessly ahead until the facts were gathered. If a witness wept or screamed or was sick to his stomach, he was urged to control his digression as quickly as possible; his interrogator, beyond a slight disdain, remained unmoved. He waited now, notebook on his lap, sleek black head resting against a flowered chintz slipcover, until one by one the Stockbridges succumbed to the power of his determination and filed from the room leaving Louise looking like a cornered rabbit.

Sergeant Putnam could not help but admire the deftness with which Lieutenant Walfield controlled the situation. George Lowell threw in a question now and then and Charles Alden made objections with predictable frequency, but the interview belonged to Lieutenant Walfield, who never changed expression as he methodically recorded items of possible interest, occasionally doing the local policemen the courtesy of asking for clarification of a point. One by one the family members took a seat in the plum-colored velveteen armchair. Louise was succeeded by a grudging Avery, a flippant Paul, a seductive Vangie, a bewildered Ellen, a helpful Henry. Malcolm arrived, raindrops pocking his gray suit coat.He was wearing his clerical collar and kept catching Charles Alden's eye as though asking, Where's your magic wand? When are you going to put an end to this?

"I realize, of course, Lieutenant, that you have to be thorough, that's a quality I treasure in myself, but surely to third-degree the members of this family is carrying the whole business too far."

"Your aunt was murdered," Lieutenant Walfield said coldly, and Malcolm flushed as he left the room.

Next came Lance, a pale, subdued Lance, and then the Strouds, Mrs., Wayne, and Annie.

"I'm sure I don't know nothing," Mrs. Stroud told them, ever helpful. "Why aren't you over to the moccasin shop asking questions of them dirty buggers in their filthy robes?"

With Chief Henderson ostentatiously matching Lieutenant Walfield note for note, Sergeant Putnam was free to observe. Letting the words wash over him, grabbing at an expression here, a nervous mannerism there, he began to form a feeling for life in this house, a picture of Eunice Stockbridge and her dictatorship.

After Wayne had slouched from the room, Lieutenant Walfield questioned Charles Alden about the matter of inheritance and, distasteful as the implication might be, Mr. Alden admitted that Paul was the chief legatee of his mother's estate.

"How much are we talking about?"

"Property, investments, I'd say we're in the neighborhood of two-and-a-half, three million. I pulled out her will last night after I had Mal's call."

Chief Henderson, who was used to wills that left five hundred dollars after debts and maybe Uncle Charlie's new band saw to Charlie Junior, actually jerked in his chair. Figures like these made him humble.

Louise Turnbull and Henry and Avery Stockbridge would receive one hundred thousand dollars apiece and the great-nieces and nephews ten thousand each. Mrs. Stockbridge's personal effects remained part of the estate except for certain pieces of jewelry which would go to the women in the family, Paul having previously inherited his father's watch, rings, and cuff links. The most valuable piece, an old-fashioned ivory hair comb set with diamonds and sapphires, was earmarked for Mary Lou.

"She can always sell it," whispered Chief Henderson, finding himself unable to picture Mary Lou at any function that called for a jeweled hair comb.

As a reward for her forty years of service, Mrs. Stroud was in line for an opal ring, Mrs. Stockbridge's thirty-year-old mink coat, and five thousand dollars. Wayne got the Buick and Annie a sable jacket.

Lieutenant Walfield had risen to his feet as he asked his final questions, indicating that his time was precious; he would leave the soothing of ruffled feathers to Charles Alden. He invited Sergeant Putnam and Chief Henderson to accompany him to interview the Blossoms of God. The fact that George Lowell remained behind reinforced the impression that his mission had less to do with prosecution than with diplomacy.

"Phew," said Chief Henderson as they swung down the driveway in the cruiser, following Lieutenant Walfield's lead, "he's an efficient bugger, you have to grant him that. My hand is just about numb. I wouldn't be surprised if he's got a fake one, made of stainless steel. Well, I'll tell you, Dave, he can have this case. Too damn many people involved. And all that money dangling out there makes a helluva good motive. Murder has been committed for a lot less than ten thousand dollars."

"The only ones who don't benefit are the Blossoms. Maybe the poor fellow *was* going to the can."

"Maybe he wasn't there at all. Avery and Malcolm were on the terrace, Mrs. Stroud in the kitchen, yet nobody else saw him. How did he get out of the house?"

"You think Louise is taking the heat off someone else?"

"Could be off herself. She was alone upstairs for an hour before Mary Lou arrived."

"Yeah, that's true."

"They were all alone at one time or another: Louise upstairs, Ellen in the woods, Henry on his walk, Avery admits he went into the house a 'couple' of times to refill his glass; he could have nipped upstairs. Malcolm could have run up when Avery was in the dining room. Lance went back to the house before Mary Lou and that's a kid I wouldn't trust to walk my dog. Then you take the Strouds. Annie's the only one in the clear. We have nothing but Mrs. Stroud's word that she stayed in the kitchen; Wayne was in and out all afternoon."

"It seems to me the only one above suspicion is Paul."

"Don't you believe it. He wasn't there, I grant you,

but the promise of a share in all that loot might easily have bought him an accomplice. I'll tell you frankly, Dave, I don't believe that there was any Blossom running down those stairs any more than I believe there was a man hanging around the grounds. I think we're going to find the answer right in Pineacres."

chapter EIGHT

The rain had kept the Blossoms from their garden but not from the chores of daily life. As the cruisers pulled into the yard of the metamorphosed shoe shop, three bedraggled young people appeared at the far end of the yard, at the edge of the woods, manhandling a cart full of logs over the root-veined earth toward a shed in front of which stood a chopping block. Two cords of split logs were stacked behind the shed, partially covered with tarpaulins. Ignoring their visitors, the Blossoms worked on stolidly in their sodden robes. Lieutenant Walfield strode toward them across a yard pocked with puddles, Chief Henderson and Sergeant Putnam squishing after him. The boys glanced at them obliquely from the corners of their eyes.

"Hey you," Walfield called.

"We do not talk to strangers," answered one, his back bent over his task. They were tossing the wet logs from the cart, which was battered and skewed with age.

"You must talk to Adoram. He is the one who talks to strangers this month. He is in the house."

"For God's sake," muttered Lieutenant Walfield, but the backs stayed bent, and after a moment, he retreated peevishly across the yard. Chief Henderson, following, winked at his colleague. It was not often they saw Lieutenant Walfield discomfited.

They stood a long time in front of the door while rain

soaked their jackets and water trickled from the eaves, drip, drip, drip, into wooden rain barrels.

Walfield banged again on the door panel and they waited some more and just as he was about to charge back across the yard, the door opened.

"I want somebody named Adoram."

"I am Adoram."

Over the boy's shoulder Sergeant Putnam caught a glimpse of the interior, which appeared like some dusky medieval alchemists's den. Logs were flickering in a stone fireplace against the far wall; over the blaze hung several blackened pots tended by three robed figures. Others were seated at a long wooden table in the center of the floor, while still others bent over some task at a second table under the windows overlooking the yard.

"May we come in?" Walfield asked.

It was a rhetorical question. His foot was already raised to clear the threshold.

Adoram said, "Strangers are not allowed inside. They disturb our equilibrium. I will talk to you in your car."

So once again they sloshed across the yard. The boy slid into the front seat with Lieutenant Walfield; Chief Henderson and Sergeant Putnam climbed into the back. Adoram was very thin, almost frail, with a shaven skull and pale blue eyes which he fixed unblinkingly on Lieutenant Walfield.

"Tell me what you know about an old lady named Mrs. Stockbridge over at the lake."

"Mrs. Stockbridge is our friend. She has kindly allowed us to use her grounds."

"For what?"

"Dancing and joyfulness."

"I see. How did you meet Mrs. Stockbridge?"

"We found her grounds an auspicious spot but her caretaker was filled with negative feelings. When he called

Mrs. Stockbridge, she said, let them dance. A few weeks later she came to stay and we thanked her."

"Mrs. Stockbridge is dead."

"I heard you."

"So maybe you won't be dancing on her lawn anymore."

"Perhaps not."

The boy's calmness which had initially impressed Sergeant Putnam as serenity soon began to seem unnatural. There was a disquieting, almost eerie quality to such a degree of self-containment.

"She died Friday afternoon while you were at Pineacres," Lieutenant Walfield told him. He might have been talking to a stone except that Adoram's blank gaze flickered over his face. "She didn't just die," he persisted harshly. "She was murdered. Someone saw one of your bunch going down the stairs inside the house."

"Then that someone is mistaken. We did not go into her house."

"Never?"

"Only Maacha went inside, the day that Mrs. Stockbridge came. It was her month to talk to strangers. I think that's all I have to say to you."

"*I* will terminate this interview," Lieutenant Walfield told him; he was definitely losing *his* equilibrium. "I want to know how long you've been here. Where did you come from?"

"We came from deceit and disharmony. We have been here one full cycle of the seasons."

"Now, listen, whatever the hell your name is, don't play games with me. When I ask where you come from, I want the name of a town."

"Such a place belongs to my former life and is no longer relevant."

"What's your real name?"

73

"Adoram."

"Your *real* name."

"Adoram."

"Your parents sure as hell didn't name you Adoram."

"I am not my parents' possession. I think we are through now."

Once again he reached for the door handle.

"You want me to take you down to the station? Because I'm just about ready to do that. When I ask you a question, I want an answer, not a riddle. Those yellow robes you all wear, where do you keep them?"

"On our bodies."

"Night and day?" Lieutenant Walfield asked, showing his distaste. "Don't you ever wash them?"

"Yes, we wash them."

"And then what do you wear? There are girls in there, aren't there?"

"We wrap ourselves in blankets."

"Don't you have a change of robes?"

"We have a few extras."

"And where are they kept?"

"In a cupboard."

"And where do you dry the wet ones?"

"Outside on a line."

"Could somebody take one?"

"Not from the line. We would be one robe short when we dressed again."

"From the cupboard?"

"How would someone take one from the cupboard unseen in a room where fifteen of us are living?"

"Don't ask me. I'm asking you."

"I must go now."

Lieutenant Walfield, with a shrug, acquiesced, but as Adoram stepped out of the cruiser, he said sharply, "You'd better do some good hard thinking, the whole

74

bunch of you. It's your word and your word only against that of our witness that you weren't in Pineacres Friday afternoon. You've just admitted that it would be damn near impossible for anyone else to take one of your robes, so if there was someone in a yellow sack running through the house last Friday, it looks like it must have been one of your group."

Adoram leaned down to speak through the open window.

"But why?" he asked softly. "Why should we want to harm a friend?"

And off he strode with considerable dignity despite his dragging robe.

"You'll be seeing me again," Lieutenant Walfield bellowed after him.

This was not the moment, Chief Henderson sensed, to attempt any light conversation. The three men shook hands and the local policemen headed homeward cheered at finding a flaw in Lieutenant Walfield's polished perfection.

"Why, hell, Dave," said Chief Henderson happily, "*Ted* could have done a better job. Can't you see old Ted standing humbly at the door with rain pouring off his bowed gray head? He'd have been inside in two minutes chatting about the weather and what kind of firewood gives the best heat, and I'll bet he'd have had the names of every one of them in half an hour."

"The *real* names," said Sergeant Putnam, and they rode on laughing like two schoolboys released from a long interview with the principal.

∗   ∗   ∗

Charles Alden stayed for dinner; George Lowell did not. Not that he was thrust out summarily into the rain. He remained with Charles Alden and the Stockbridges for some time after the departure of the policemen, discussing the situation and its implications and was furnished with a glass of quite drinkable sherry. But a second glass was not forthcoming. As the invisible line was crossed between business and pleasure, he found himself on his way to the door, with Malcolm an affable escort, entrusting him to carry to the district attorney the family's expressions of gratitude for his personal attention.

Henry had by this time staggered into the living room with several armloads of kindling and logs and a fire was blazing brightly in the massive stone fireplace which lent a measure of cheer to the gathering, although as a source of warmth it proved ineffectual in that cavernous chamber. Ellen pulled an armchair close to the flames; Malcolm took a seat flanking the couch which Louise and Avery shared with Charles Alden. The sherry, the fire, and their blessed native, ingrained self-assurance dispelled the lingering aftertaste of Lieutenant Walfield's rudeness.

Charles Alden assured them that the inquest was simply a formality. He comforted them with the philosophy that although Aunt Eunice had died under tragic circumstances, life must go on. He informed them that in his experience this kind of case often remained unsolved and after a brief initial flurry of interest, the media soon withdrew. It appeared to him an incident of random violence, a sign of the times they lived in, when *no one* was safe; the Stockbridges gravely contemplated this lack of respect by the lower classes.

Paul and Vangie had disappeared on the heels of Mr. Lowell, compelled by blatant lust. They had, during the morning's proceedings, been struck by one of those moods of mutual sexual excitement that make every glance deliciously suggestive and they were up the stairs before the door had decently closed, counting on Charles

Alden's presence to keep their elders by the fireside. In their headlong romp up the stairway they overtook a plodding Mary Lou engaged in a quest for serenity and solitude.

"Shit," muttered Mary Lou, as their laughter floated back to her from the third-floor hallway. Her boxy little sanctuary under the eaves had just been placed off-limits by her own fastidiousness; although she'd like to see *anyone* achieve peace of mind with gasps and giggles and the sound of bouncing bedsprings coming from across the hall. She found the image of those sleek brown limbs depressing. There were certain volumes in the bookstore where she worked that featured some remarkable photographic essays and these Mary Lou had perused hastily when alone in the shop, reaching the discouraging conclusion that this was an act for a contortionist in abundant good health. Firm tummies, lithe limbs, tight buttocks abounded. Where were the little fat people? Were they excluded from these rituals?

Trapped, she stood on the second-floor landing, prevented by her sensibilities from climbing higher and loath to go lower to be met with exasperated pity from her kinfolk and dark looks from Mrs. Stroud, who shared the family feeling that Mary Lou had let a misplaced sense of duty misguide her.

Don't go looking for trouble was one of Mrs. Stroud's favorite maxims, and Mary Lou was in no mood to appreciate either those or similar words of wisdom.

It came to her that the sewing room might offer refuge until dinnertime and she headed in that direction. The door to Louise and Malcolm Turnbull's bedroom was slightly ajar and as she passed, her ear caught a sound, a sharp clink twice repeated, as of a glass set down or two bottles touching. Curiosity fought with the horror of coming face to face with Aunt Eunice's murderer in the act of . . . well, what? Impatiently she thrust the door boldly open and caught Lance standing by his parents' mahogany bureau going through his mother's purse.

"Oh, it's you, Lou," he said, continuing his search. "Jeez, you gave me a start. What are you creeping around for? Looking for another corpse? No, I didn't mean that; it's awful about Graunty. And you were the one that figured it out, huh? Clever Lou. Hell, the old lady's as broke as I am."

And he set the purse back in its place on the top of the bureau and followed Mary Lou from the room.

"Boy, you sure stirred things up," he said admiringly. "I think you beat my old record for stirring up which was set on the eve of my departure from Bowdoin."

"So what would you have done?" snapped Mary Lou.

"Oh, stirred," Lance agreed. "Stirred like mad, dear cousin. I find it hard to believe, though, don't you, Lou, that Graunty was bumped off? That doesn't affect the inheritance, does it?" he added anxiously.

"Only if you did it."

"You shouldn't say a thing like that. That hatchet-faced cop wouldn't need much excuse to drag me down to the station and apply the rubber hoses. Ten thousand dollars, Lou, isn't that what old Beaky said? Ten thousand buckeroos. I'm on my way to L.A.," he sang, taking a few whirling dance steps down the hall. "I wonder when we get it. I quit my job yesterday or, as Pop would say, I resigned my present position. I'd rather be out here where the action is. Hey, you got any ideas, cuz? Give me the inside scoop. You think those Blossoms did it?"

"No."

"Neither do I. Those kids are good honest freaks; they're not vicious. How about the guy you saw hanging around outside?"

"Nobody takes him seriously."

"Why not? The mysterious stranger? What could be better from the family's point of view? That's where we will concentrate our efforts, Lou. Hey, I'm on my way to L.A. What are you going to do with your money, you wild spendthrift?"

"Bury it."

Lance laughed. "What a lousy day, huh? We can't even go down to old Scum Pond. So what happens next?"

"Inquest. Tuesday morning. Funeral Wednesday at two."

"And then they pass out the checks, huh? Don't you think it's ironic, Lou, that I am now a thousandaire and have not a penny in my pockets? I don't suppose you . . ."

"You suppose right," said Mary Lou repressively as Mrs. Stroud's nasal dinner announcement rose from the nether regions.

Lance spun around to answer the summons.

"Where's our lovebirds?" he asked, clattering down the back stairway.

"In their love nest," Mary Lou said sourly, falling in behind.

*　　*　　*

By the time Charles Alden left in midafternoon the household had returned almost to normalcy. Intense emotion could not be sustained indefinitely and the unpleasant conjectures of the last forty-eight hours had given way to a gentle air of thoughtfulness appropriate to the natural passing of an aged relative, the reality of the situation being unconsciously proscribed. The afternoon's interlude came very close to contentment, due in part to the quite natural secret contemplation of Aunt Eunice's beneficence, prematurely revealed, and in part, quite frankly, to her absence.

Aunt Eunice in the abstract was far easier to love than Aunt Eunice in the flesh. The clouds might be thickening outside the long rain-spattered windows but the skies had definitely brightened within. Long stretches of quiet time went by free of sly observations concerning declining church attendance or the high incidence of drug use in the U.S. Army. Mrs. Stroud was spared the preparation of the tea tray and Mary Lou its delivery. Ellen Stockbridge was free to slap down her cards in open defiance of the Sabbath, and it was a measure of the collective mood that Mary Lou played interminable games of gin rummy with her mother as though a breach had never occurred. Indeed, Malcolm felt affairs well enough in hand to pack his suitcase and return briefly to parish duties, planning to reappear in time for the inquest Tuesday morning. On Wednesday, with suitable devotion, they would lay Aunt Eunice to rest and Thursday they would meet in Charles Alden's office for the formal reading of her will, the revelation of whose contents was proving so much food for fantasy this afternoon.

Paul had just begun to realize, in somewhat of a daze, that he was personally wealthy, and struggled to damp down an elation which seemed incompatible with his genuine grief. He had never experienced the heavy hand of his mother's domination because he had refused to meet her on anything more than a superficial level, and by seeing her only at infrequent intervals had maintained illusions on both sides. Vangie was eminently adaptable to his moods, planning the disposal of his wealth with one breath, albeit with repressed excitement in deference to the fact of death, and consoling him the next moment for the loss of his Mom, and as the roles were equally gratifying, the afternoon was not ill spent.

*　　*　　*

Chief Henderson and Sergeant Putnam had, in the mean-
time, returned to the station to find Ted dozing peacefully, hands folded in his lap, upper plate quivering
precipitously. He awoke without embarrassment, refreshed and bright eyed, and having reminded Chief
Henderson that the last two hours qualified as overtime,
he bid them a genial goodbye and ambled homeward.

"Two o'clock," said Chief Henderson, poised in the
doorway. "I didn't know it was so late. That damned
little dried-up roast beef will be sitting there as a monument to my tardiness. Look at that rain come down.
Probably washing out my pea seeds. The first planting
froze, the crows ate the second. I tell you, Dave, you
have to be a masochist to garden in New England."

And with that gloomy observation, he plunged into
the streaming rain, leaving Sergeant Putnam a quiet office
for a shift that was notoriously the slowest of a slow day.

chapter NINE

A short diversion was provided by Barbara and Jenny bearing sandwiches and coffee in answer to his urgent plea. When mother and daughter had departed in matching blue slickers, Sergeant Putnam turned his attention to the processing of accumulated paperwork without achieving his usual sense of virtue. There were two days of patient response represented by these reports, an array of emotions concealed behind the formal language that spanned the whole human tragedy; Dinky Poo, Mrs. Johnson's Siamese cat, missing three nights; little Billy Taggert's brand-new 10-speed bike, purchased with the profits of his paper route, audaciously snatched right off the Taggerts' screened porch; "Mr. Glass Sucks," spray-painted on the west wall of the high school. Such was his preoccupation with, or his seduction by, a "real" crime that he would gladly have swept the whole pile on the floor and forgotten it. Up and down he bobbed for nothing more important than a glance at the empty puddled parking lot, and by four o'clock was so impatient with himself and his mood that he greeted with relief the arrival of a visitor who, under normal circumstances, engendered mixed feelings.

Bea Lambert was an aging maiden lady who had played a not inconsiderable part in the solution of Hampford's recent homicides. She had lived all her life on Eagle Hill in a house that had been her grandfather's and what Bea didn't know about Hampford could be put on the head of a pin; she possessed, as Sergeant Putnam had learned the hard way, a finely honed skill at extracting the most confidential material. His acquaintance with Bea dated from a fourth-grade Sunday school class to which Bea introduced Moses and Abraham with the graciousness of a Welcome Wagon hostess. A broken engagement was alluded to now and then; family duties had intervened. Bea had nursed her father through his final illness and had then taken on the role of companion to her bereft mother, who had lingered on healthily for another thirty years.

"Well, David," she said cheerfully, shaking drops of water from dear Father's (God rest his soul) black umbrella with the parrot handle, which was now somewhat more purple than black, and setting it to dry by the door, "isn't this a wet old day. The kind of day on which a body seeks a little company. Are you all alone?"

As if you didn't know, thought Sergeant Putnam wryly. Bea was attired in her Sunday afternoon dress which to the uninitiated might appear identical to her Sunday morning dress; it was, in fact, one year older. Because of the inclement weather she was wearing plastic garden boots and a fluffy home-knit cardigan that lent her the appearance of a fuzzy peach.

"Ted's off duty," Sergeant Putnam told her, coming around the counter to escort her to one of the plastic bucket chairs and taking a seat himself on the opposite side of the coffee table whose water-marked surface appeared to exist for the sole purpose of offering up one cheap china ashtray.

"Len went home for dinner and Everett's on vacation."

"He usually is," Bea said dryly, smoothing her skirt and settling herself as composedly as though she were taking tea in the best parlor. Preliminaries were important to Bea and it was a measure of the immensity of the day's news when she cut them short.

"David," she told him somberly, shaking her gray curls, "I am stunned by Eunice Stockbridge's method of passing on. Our little town will soon be known as the murder capital of the world."

"I don't think it's reached epidemic proportions yet, Bea, but I agree it's pretty sobering to find that we are not immune to violence."

Bea's knowledge of the tragedy at Pineacres did not in the least surprise him. Too many townspeople had an Aunt Elsie at the switchboard of Mount Pleasant Hospital or a cousin Ralph mopping floors at Wall and Sons to keep secret for long an occasion of illness or death. Their most spirited community activity was the assembling from fragments of information a coherent whole.

"I suppose she'll be buried in Boston. I'd like to attend the funeral as a mark of respect for the family. I didn't know Eunice well, but dear Father and Henry Francis, Winthrop's father, were friends for years, and I am very familiar with Pineacres, indeed I am. You see, in those days, David, five or six big summer houses shared the lake, none of these little cottages that have crept in since, and those five or six families came out for the whole summer: mothers, children, maids, dogs, and maiden aunts, and what a leisurely life they led with dips in the lake, lots of canoeing, charades, and croquet. Pineacres had a lawn tennis court, people played on grass then, you know, and it must have taken one full-time gardener to keep that court in good condition.

"In any case, somehow Father struck up an acquaintance with Henry Stockbridge, I suppose it was a meeting of like minds, and two or three times a summer for many years, we three girls and Mother and Father would spend a day at Pineacres. We were not allowed out on the water as Mother had a dear friend whose only son drowned in a boating accident. Swimming was also forbidden, Mother's youngest sister, Alice, having died of tuberculosis at twenty, brought on, the family always believed, by a chill taken after swimming. Mother had a horror of our going the same way, poor dear, although as events proved, she feared the wrong disease. It was cancer that took our Dorothy."

"You didn't mind not swimming? My kids would have a fit."

"As a matter of fact, we didn't. Mother had so imbued us with her own fears that we regarded the lake as a very malevolent body of water indeed. We played very happily on dry land with Georgie Stockbridge, enjoying his wonderful playroom or rambling through the woods.

"Winthrop and his brother Francis were young men then, Francis the elder by two years and always the center of a crowd of young people. How he loved to play tennis! Whenever I think of Francis Stockbridge, I think of him flushed and laughing in his tennis whites. Oh, it seems like only yesterday, David, that he made a little girl's heart beat faster. He became Louise and Henry's father," she explained, "and died young for all his liveliness, dropped dead in the middle of a serve. Winthrop was quieter, a little staid, even as a young man, and no match for his brother in my opinion, but a good boy and very considerate of his mother. They had their sorrows, that family did. They lost their only girl, their little Edith, before I was born, and Harold, the third brother, suffered a ruptured appendix and died in two days at the age of thirteen. That was a not uncommon cause of death in the days before antibiotics, you know. It was a terrible blow to the family; he was a cheerful bright boy, much like his brother Francis.

"George was the baby and our playmate, as he was the

only one close to us in age; in fact, he and Dorothy shared the same birth date. He grew up to be a pilot in the Second World War and was killed at the age of thirty. Avery is his son. He was an infant when his father died which may account in part for the path he's taken.

"So there you are, David," Bea said pensively, gazing back down the tunnel of time to a sunlit lawn and the crack of croquet mallets and a solemn little boy in a sailor suit pelting with acorns the white-clad Lambert sisters whose corkscrew curls bounced like springs. "They grew up and we grew up and Henry Francis and dear Father passed on and I lost direct contact with the family. But that early acquaintance and those happy times gave me a lasting interest in their affairs and I've always relished any news of Pineacres and the Stockbridges."

"When did Eunice come on the scene?"

"Just after the war. I met her the last time I was out there, on a visit with Mother to see Winthrop's mother, Bertha; she was not well. In fact, she died the next winter; she never really recovered from George's death. Winthrop was there with his new wife. She was a beautiful woman, very poised, but not in quite the same class as the Stockbridges and grating on Henry and Bertha, you could see that. Mother said to me on the way home, 'Bea,' she said, 'that house is not big enough for both of them.' But Winthrop was as besotted as men often are who marry late. They were both over forty, you know; she'd been married before, at least once. I think if she could have given him a child, he would have been in heaven. But nothing happened along those lines although they tried and tried."

"How do you know how hard they tried?" Sergeant Putnam asked with a grin, causing Bea to blush.

"I had my sources," she said firmly. "Mrs. Stroud's mother, Blanche, was the Stockbridge's cook and

Blanche's second cousin Elmira was doing Mother's heavy cleaning once a week and I don't believe I've ever in my entire life come across such a talker as Elmira Stroud; she was a perfect gold mine. So you see I knew what was going on, that they had been to doctors and there didn't seem to be anything wrong but Eunice did not conceive and soon she was too old to bear a child and it seemed that they were resigned to that fact. Then Francis died, in 1952, his father having preceded him by a year or two, and goodness, if that didn't stir everything up again. Becoming the oldest son and heir seemed to intensify Winthrop's longing for a son of his own and the next thing we knew they had adopted Paul."

"Paul's adopted?"

"You didn't think Eunice gave birth to him at fifty-two, did you?"

"I didn't work out the ages," Sergeant Putnam admitted humbly. "But, good Lord, Bea, what agency would give a baby to fifty-year-old parents?"

"None," said Bea. "It was a private placement."

"You mean through a lawyer or a doctor?"

"Something like that."

"You wouldn't know which or who?"

"I'm afraid I don't," Bea had to admit. "Mrs. Stroud might have known, not Estelle, but her mother, Blanche. Paul's nursemaid came from Boston with him for the summer and she might have let something drop to Mrs. Stroud, if she knew anything to drop, or maybe to Noreen, Estelle's sister. She worked up there, too, I believe, and she's still around. But I don't know what this has to do with Eunice's death. Paul was doted upon by his father and spoiled by his mother. They gave him everything. He'd have no reason to kill her."

"He's become a very wealthy young man."

"But he never lacked for anything, David. If I had to put my money on a family member, I'd choose Avery."

"You don't like Avery?"

"My personal feelings do not enter into my choice. The fact is, Avery Stockbridge needs money. He's been kept on at his law firm despite his drinking—Peabody, Peabody, Stockbridge and Peabody—only, I suspect, because a Stockbridge alleviates all those Peabodys. But he's paying alimony to at least two ex-wives and is at any given time either getting into or out of some expensive affair."

"Hmmm."

"None of them is as well off as you might think from appearances. The Stockbridge name is as solid as ever, but financially, affairs took a plummet under old Henry. While he was denouncing the automobile as a passing fad, the Stockbridge harness company quietly expired. He left real estate, mostly, to his sons, which Winthrop managed cautiously and profitably. But George, of course, died young, before he came into his inheritance, and Francis did not possess his brother's frugal spirit. He lived right up to his income and then some. Moreover, whatever he had to pass along was passed thirty years ago.

"Now, I'm not saying they're in *distress*. I'm sure that Henry has a little something besides his pension and Louise is not entirely dependent on that minister husband of hers, but neither do they have enough for that big extra, whatever it might be."

"Which one hundred thousand dollars would supply."

"Well, wouldn't it? And then there's also the question of jealousy. Avery may well feel cheated because his father did not receive his inheritance. Even though his grandfather put Avery through school, perhaps Avery thinks he ought to have had more. And how do Francis's children feel? Do Henry and Louise realize that their father squandered the same inheritance that their Uncle Winthrop nurtured, or do they feel that somehow their Uncle Winthrop was unfairly favored? Goodness, David, if we could only peer inside people's minds."

"I'm rather glad we can't, Bea. As it is you scare me with the amount of information you dredge up."

Bea smiled complacently and immediately confirmed his fears.

"Where do the Blossoms fit into this?"

"What makes you think they fit in anywhere?"

"Because you and Len and Lieutenant Walfield went to see them this afternoon. And there is nothing the least bit mysterious about my knowing of that visit, David. With the three of you milling around in the mud puddles and our cruiser and Walfield's cruiser parked right in the middle of the yard, it would be strange if I *didn't* hear about it. Of course, it's none of my business what you were doing out there."

"It really isn't," Sergeant Putnam agreed with a smile.

Bea smiled back. "I've enjoyed our little talk," she told him, with a glance at the wall clock, "and I'm sure it's been healthier for you than sitting here alone listening to the rain come down. That kind of thing leads to depression."

"Don't rush off, Bea. I want to know something about the Strouds."

"Oh goodness, the Strouds have been at Pineacres as long as the Stockbridges. Mrs. Stroud's great-grandmother was cook for Charles William, who built the house."

So that was the C.W., thought Sergeant Putnam, who had so egocentrically embellished the entrance to his property.

" . . . and all the staff when I went there as a child, and

there were many more of them then, of course, were dark-complected people. They like to allude to gypsy blood, but frankly, David, it's plain old Indian. Dogtown holds the remnants of the Wompanaki tribe."

"Why is it called Dogtown?"

"I've always *hoped,*" said Bea, "that the name refers simply to a large population of man's best friend. Perhaps I'd rather not know. There was an ugly and pervasive prejudice against the area when I was growing up. I think we've come some way since then."

"Is it reservation land?"

"No, it's part of the township of Sheffield. The Wompanakis were a third-rate tribe at best, absorbed by stronger tribes years and years ago. They can't even file a lawsuit; they have nothing to reclaim. Conditions have never been better than pretty awful. The lucky families are those who have regular summer people."

"The Strouds are considered pretty well off then?"

"My goodness, they're *all* Strouds; there's hardly a soul out here that doesn't bear the name. If you mean our Mrs. Stroud, yes, I think she is, comparatively speaking of course."

"Does our Mrs. Stroud have a husband?"

"You might say so. He's been in and out of prison for years. The last sentence he received was a very stiff one because he did something extremely nasty; he tied up a store clerk so tightly, with a noose around his neck, that the poor fellow suffered brain damage. Luckily, Estelle had the Pineacres job and as the children grew older, she got them working there, too. There was a boy killed in Vietnam, I believe, and a couple of other children. They're good soldiers, you know; they discovered a source of pride in their young men during the First World War and a disproportionately large number of Dogtown citizens have fought and died in every war since.

"Now, David, I do believe the rain has slackened and I must be on my way. I'm going up to see Essie, who is having one of her bad spells. She'll expect me to have a few tidbits of news to brighten her day, poor soul."

She paused at the top of the stairs to raise her umbrella. Rain was no longer falling but the heavy-coated maples were shaking off surplus drops.

"I had a nice chat with Barbara the other day," said Bea. "We met in front of the hardware store where she was buying picture hangers to put up the mirror you got at the yard sale which you said was a piece of junk but Barbara knew was an antique and sure enough when she got the paint off it proved to be cherry."

"I'm not infallible."

"I've never dared to ask her this, David, but just what does a teacher's aide do?"

"All the things the teacher doesn't want to do," said Sergeant Putnam with a grin.

"You know I'm very glad Barbara has the job and I'm sure that she's an excellent teacher's aide, but my stars, David, I wonder if we're not giving children today too much aid. Why, in my day, we not only did our lessons and our homework but the boys filled the woodbox and we girls dusted and swept the schoolroom every morning, and I don't believe our psyches were damaged. But perhaps it's better to be a little more helpless nowadays. With all the machines we have to do everything for us, if a body was self-sufficient, he'd be no help to the economy at all. I expect the best American nowadays is your most incompetent one, so I guess we're raising good citizens after all."

"It's certainly food for thought, Bea."

"It will give you something to mull over this afternoon," Bea told him, descending the stairs. Sergeant Putnam shut the door with a smile. He had quite a bit to mull over, thanks to Bea.

chapter TEN

Monday morning dawned pale golden, the sky a fragile blue as though washed to the point of fading by Sunday's rain. Drops of water clung to the creamy blossoms of the climbing roses that flanked Sergeant Putnam's kitchen door and in Barbara's flower border along the driveway, an Oriental poppy had opened its crinkled papery petals, a bold exotic interloper in a staid New England garden.

Arms swinging, he strode down Summer Street, breathing lungfuls of the perfumed, earthy air. The grass on the common shone coarse and vibrant, the bright green of a child's drawing. General Cyrus Higgenbottom, cast in bronze on a bronze steed and freshly washed of pigeon droppings, gazed down benignly on his passing figure.

In front of the Town Hall, in two wooden half-barrels, petunias planted by the garden club were struggling to raise their mud-spattered blossoms of red, white, and purple, while the flag that had served as the inspiration for this color scheme rippled on its pole above the front door.

Sergeant Putnam climbed the steps at the side of the building beneath the neon sign that spelled POLICE and skated across a highly waxed floor that meant Ted was on duty. Through Chief Henderson's open door, he caught a glimpse of his boss on the phone, grinning and gesticulating.

"Something good happen?"

"I'd be the last to know," said Ted, raising his mournful brown eyes from the pencil sharpener. "I'm awfully glad you've come, Dave. I've got to get over to Walnut Street. I think Mrs. Johnson's Siamese has been found in a culvert. I'd like to break the news to her personally."

"I understand, Ted."

Ted's empathy with his animal friends was a recognized and respected aspect of his character.

"Ralph Hubbard came across the body when he was cleaning out a storm drain that got jammed up with debris in yesterday's rain," Ted told him sorrowfully, shuffling back to his desk with a fistful of needle-sharp pencils. "I'm afraid there's no doubt that it's Dinky Poo. He was wearing his little blue collar with the bell. He's not an outdoor animal normally, you see; those are the ones that get confused when they do escape. They don't have any road sense. I hope he didn't suffer, didn't crawl in there . . . and lie there . . . alone."

"Well, you hustle right along, Ted," Sergeant Putnam urged him, as Ted, too choked up to continue, slapped his cap on his head and padded out of the station, just as Chief Henderson erupted from his office with a great big grin.

"Guess what?"

"Just tell me."

"The Stockbridge family," said Chief Henderson, with sly delight, "have requested that the local police department handle the case. They didn't take to Walfield—well, that was obvious—and as for Lowell, he's completely out of it; apparently he's some kind of social impostor. Anyway, they don't want Lowell, they don't want Walfield, they want us!"

"Wow."

"Of course, the thought did cross my mind," Chief Henderson added, turning quite sober, "that they requested us not for our competency but for our lack of it; that is, they hope that if we're on the case, nothing will happen."

"For God's sake, Len," said Sergeant Putnam in exasperation, "I'll bet you were the kind of kid who volunteered for left field."

"And just because they don't want Walfield," Chief Henderson continued, ignoring him, "doesn't mean that Walfield is not going to be involved."

"But not up front."

"Well, no. He'll keep in the background and give us plenty of rope to hang ourselves with. Come in, come in, the door's open."

A shadow appeared against the screen, fracturing the neat rectangle of sunlight imprinted on the gleaming tile floor. The door swung forward a cautious inch or two, a pause, then inward another foot and Adoram slipped noiselessly into the room on bony, scarred feet and stood with his back against the wall looking like a frail trapped bird; the robe, slipping from his thin shoulders, revealed jutting collarbones.

"You want to talk to us?"

"Yes."

"Damn," said Chief Henderson. "I've got a meeting in five minutes with Myron Streeter, our perennial selectman and would-be dictator. You think you can handle this, Dave?"

Sergeant Putnam swallowed his annoyance at the question, which he had learned over time to regard not as a slur on his competency but as an indicator, as sensitive as a barometric reading, of Len's anxiety level.

"Come sit down," he invited Adoram, waving a hand toward the plastic chairs. "You walk all the way?"

"Part of the way."

No small talk here. Adoram sat as motionless as a lizard, moving only his eyes, and falling under the scrutiny of his pale gaze, Sergeant Putnam began to empathize with Lieutenant Walfield. It took all his self-control not to fidget.

"I have something to tell you."

"I'm listening."

"When you policemen left our property yesterday, I explained to the rest of our group the reasons for your presence. When I asked about a missing robe, Abimelech, who was in charge of laundry last week, said that one day, and he is quite sure it was Friday, he discovered not a missing robe but an extra one. Or thinks he did. He did not count the robes when he hung them out. We do not concern ourselves overly much with the number of our possessions; such trivial matters are incompatible with spiritual soaring. If we do not have enough robes we make more."

I'll bet *you* don't make them, thought Sergeant Putnam irrelevantly. I'll bet anything, that life being what it is, the girls are hacking out these garments. And he pictured their greasy locks bent over ancient treadle machines.

"But it was his impression," said Adoram, "that the line had not been full to the tree in the morning and it was at night. So it is possible that the robe was pinned to the line."

"Is this line in clear view of the house?"

"The near end of it is. The far end is behind bushes."

"So that a robe might have been taken at some time in the same way?"

"It's possible."

"But you never noticed the loss?"

"No."

"Let me ask you something, Adoram. Do you ever see anyone hanging around your property who doesn't belong there?"

"Boys come sometimes on dirt bikes to ride through the yard, and people on snowmobiles, even though the land is posted. Sometimes one of Mrs. Stockbridge's nephews comes to watch us, the short one."

"Hmmmm."

"He does no harm. We would give him whatever information he wishes, but he would rather peek at us from behind the trees."

"You didn't happen to notice him peeking last Friday, did you?"

"I myself did not happen to see him but I will ask the others."

"Thank you, Adoram. I appreciate your coming in to talk to us."

"We would like to be of assistance," Adoram told him, rising. "We are sad about Mrs. Stockbridge; she was good to us."

And sidestepping the table, he glided to the door and disappeared down the stairs with the lightness of a wraith.

Chief Henderson returned ten minutes later, looking pleased with himself.

"So what did Myron want?"

"*Ostensibly* he wanted to see me about my complaint concerning his lordly assumption that every time he books a group into the Eastey House he has the right to make a traffic cop out of any convenient member of my department, off duty or on. He's got the place so heavily scheduled, we could well be running shorthanded all summer. I especially wanted to get to him before next weekend and Sunday's tea for the Descendants of the Illegitimate Sons and Daughters of the Kings of Britain."

"Lord, yes," Sergeant Putnam agreed. "That's a volatile group. Last year we had a fistfight in the rose garden."

96

"However," said Chief Henderson, "despite my urgency, not a word was heard until this morning when suddenly he couldn't wait to see me. And not surprisingly, and not at all subtly, the conversation soon turned to events at Pineacres. He seems to hold me personally responsible for the increase in homicides; I wouldn't be surprised if I didn't have to stand up at the next town meeting and make a public apology."

Sergeant Putnam laughed.

"But he paid, Dave, he paid for every scrap of information. We're going to have the Boy Scouts take over traffic control which means we get off the hook and Myron doesn't have to pay a cent; it all comes under the heading of good deeds. So it's full speed ahead for the Colonial Dames and the Piscataqua Pioneers. Now what did our young Blossom have to tell us?"

"Some tale about a robe turning up on their line last Friday which they never missed in the first place."

"Oh brother, this robe is getting quite a workout. Proves they're not as simple as they let on."

"He also told me they've spotted Henry Stockbridge in their woods on occasion, apparently watching them. Adoram will ask if anyone saw him last Friday."

"Of course, somebody will have seen him last Friday, Dave. Use your head. They've come up with the same old stratagem that Louise Stockbridge did, but taken it one step further."

"No harm in finding out why Henry's been over there."

"Hell, no. Go ask him. I'm going into my office and heat up that phone. Let's see what we can dredge up about our Stockbridges, discreetly of course. Myron warned me against coming on too heavy-handed. It seems that Pineacres represents a helluva lot of tax

97

money. Oh, what I wouldn't give to work in a vacuum. Where's Ted? Take him along."

"He's holding Mrs. Johnson's hand. Dinky Poo has gone to kitty heaven."

"Oh, for God's sake. Get over there and break up the wake."

chapter ELEVEN

The trip to Pineacres was enlivened by Ted's reminiscences of dogs and cats he had known in thirty years of service to the four-legged citizens of Hampford. There was old Blackie, rescued from a dry-well, who still hobbled out, fifteen years later, to lick Ted's hand in gratitude whenever he passed; cats plucked from telephone poles, trees, housetops, and chimneys; Bubba, a mammoth ringtail, lured from his perch on the Town Hall flagpole with bits of bologna from Ted's lunchbox. Ted chuckled at their foibles as the landscape flashed past, his cap resting on his eyebrows and his large hairy ears.

The moccasin shop appeared less forlorn on this balmy day but also less permanent, its structural defects mercilessly illuminated by the noonday sun. Once again the garden was under attack by a swarm of hoe-wielding, yellow-robed individuals of both sexes. Ted clicked his tongue and shook his head and made his disapproval manifest.

"What do you have against them, Ted? They don't do any harm."

"Excuse me, Dave, but they do. They startle the wits out of our senior citizens. Ginny Armstrong was telling me just the other day that her old father came home all shaken, thought he'd seen an apparition; the pleasure is gone from his daily walk, poor soul. And living there all together," Ted said, lowering his voice, "male and female

indiscriminately . . . how can they call themselves a religious community when they're living in sin?"

"Hmmmm."

"You take a youngster, Dave, his parents have bought
shoes for that kid and winter jackets and paid for braces
and contact lenses and hockey camp, and pushed him into
school and pulled him into church, made something out
of him *despite* himself, then they send him off to college
or out to work and just when it looks like they might
begin to cash in, a subversive bunch like this one seduces
him to quit his job or drop out of school to go back to a
way of life that our grandparents fought like hell to get
out of. It's a setback for the whole middle class," said Ted
gloomily.

And he remained uncharacteristically silent until the
sight of the Pineacres entrance pillars jolted him into the
recollection of a long-ago Fourth of July parade in which
George Stockbridge won first prize driving a red, white,
and blue chariot behind a horse with gold harness.

"Of course it wasn't *real* gold," Ted added punc-
tiliously.

Sergeant Putnam swung into the loop of the driveway,
glancing automatically toward the garage, but Wayne and
the Buick were absent from their accustomed spot. In
fact, the parking area was so sparsely occupied it appeared that many of the weekend visitors had returned to
normal life.

Followed by an avidly curious Ted, he led the way
down the walk to the front of the house where Lance and
Mary Lou were engaged in a halfhearted game of croquet. As they approached, Mary Lou gave her ball a
vicious swipe that sent it spinning six inches to the side.
She raised a pudgy arm in greeting, as Lance said wearily,
"C'mon, Lou, I've gone around three times."

Louise Stockbridge, watching them from the shade of

the umbrella on the terrace, notebook open at her right hand, did not express any pleasure at the arrival of more policemen. She was clearly harassed by the duties pressing in upon her and resentful that funeral plans must remain indefinite until after the inquest. Her husband, she told them in reply to Sergeant Putnam's questions, had returned to parish business for the day, Ellen Stockbridge was shopping for a dress for the funeral, Avery was running errands in town, and Paul and Vangie were attempting to soothe Vangie's parents who were understandably dismayed at the specter of homicide hovering over their prospective in-laws.

"But of course someone didn't think of that," Louise said acidly, looking daggers at Mary Lou, who was on her hands and knees retrieving her ball from beneath a spreading yew.

"Is your brother around?"

"Mary Lou," her aunt called automatically, and Mary Lou, who had been playing with an eye to the terrace, put down her mallet and stood beneath the geraniums, her glasses steamed with perspiration. Ted dragged his gaze from Louise and focused greedily on Mary Lou as though he were collecting specimens of Stockbridges.

"Do you know where your father is?"

"I think he's gone walking, Aunt Louise."

"Could you find him?"

"Not if he doesn't want to be found. How are you?" she asked Sergeant Putnam. "Are you making progress?"

"I like to think we are. This is Officer Deegan, Mary Lou."

Ted blushed and twisted his cap. Mary Lou sat down on the stone steps, a dumpy figure in a striped tank top and red nylon shorts. Lance cast a glance of disgust at the terrace and began to whack croquet balls as though he were playing golf.

"It's a beautiful spot," Sergeant Putnam observed, leaning back in his chair and gazing over the verdant lawn and the sparkling lake whose surface betrayed no hint of the muck beneath.

"All Paul's now, is it? No question of the legality of his inheritance, I suppose. He *was* legally adopted?"

Louise shot him a startled glance and gazed at him appraisingly before she replied. Perhaps Len was right, thought Sergeant Putnam, in which case her expectations of a superficial investigation could not help but be shaken somewhat by the knowledge that the family background had been under surveillance.

"Of course he was," she said shortly, making quite clear her repugnance at the crudity of his questions. But Sergeant Putnam showed little respect for upper-class fastidiousness.

"How old was Paul when they got him?" he bored on, riding roughshod over Louise's sensitivity.

"He was practically newborn," Louise answered testily, succumbing to his persistence and responding also perhaps to the fact that her audience had expanded. Mary Lou was listening with interest and Lance, tiring of his solitary game, had joined his cousin on the steps. Louise capitulated.

"I was twenty-two years old when Paul came," she told Sergeant Putnam. "Malcolm and I had been married for a year and I was expecting Bryon. We were living in Pennsylvania where Malcolm had his first parish and I don't think I even got home for Christmas that year. But of course my mother let me know at once. She could hardly wait to call."

"Were you surprised?"

"Flabbergasted would be a better word. But happy. They had wanted a child so badly. And Paul was such a darling. I saw him for the first time the following summer when I came up here for a month with Bryon. After all, I wanted to show off my baby, too. And they were awfully sweet together, one so blond and the other so dark."

"I suppose Paul had a nursemaid."

"Oh yes, a very competent woman from Boston. The whole household revolved around Paul. He was completely spoiled by everyone from his mother to old Augusta in the kitchen."

"I thought her name was Blanche."

"Blanche was her daughter. Augusta was my grandparents' cook, retiring in favor of Blanche at my grandfather's death in 1952. But Blanche was in poor health and unreliable and our Mrs. Stroud was only a girl. So Augusta came back for several years; I suppose she was afraid the job would go out of the family. She worked until she was at least seventy and then our Mrs. Stroud relieved her and has been with us ever since."

"Where did Paul come from?"

"He was the child of the daughter of my aunt and uncle's closest friends, something like that, and he was left an orphan and they were asked to take him."

"Why didn't his grandparents keep him?"

"His grandmother was dying of cancer."

"I see."

Louise laughed. "Now really, Sergeant, you can't possibly see any significance in that. I'm afraid this whole line of questioning is going to prove quite unprofitable. Paul may be as dark as a Stroud but I assure you, he is legally as much a Stockbridge as I am."

"I think Dad's home," said Mary Lou.

A door slammed as though in confirmation of her observation. Footsteps resounded in the echoing hallway and Henry Stockbridge strode onto the terrace dressed in a black turtleneck jersey and neatly creased chinos.

"Well, Sergeant, back again I see," he greeted them cheerily, shaking hands briskly with both men. "Saw your cruiser in the yard. What can I do for you?"

"I'd like a few words with you privately, sir, if you don't mind."

"Not at all."

Henry beamed at what he obviously interpreted as an appeal to his unique talents.

"Always ready to oblige. Excuse us, Louise."

"Gladly," Louise said tartly, and gathering up her notebook she departed toward the house. Lance rose to his feet with greater reluctance, hauling Mary Lou up after him.

"Banished to the playing fields, cuz," he told her. "You cannot escape your destiny."

Mary Lou stumbled after him hardly conscious of her actions. Through her mind reverberated Sergeant Putnam's introduction: "This is Officer Deegan, Mary Lou." Not Miss Stockbridge, but Mary Lou. Did he call her mother Ellen, her father Henry, her Uncle Malcolm Mal? He did not. She alone was the recipient of this intimate form of address. Mary Lou! It sounded almost pretty, this name that rhymed with phew and poo.

Ridiculous, said her brain cells, but her heart beat pit-a-pat, and the warm glow radiating outward from this palpitating organ, coupled with the fact that Sergeant Putnam's gaze was fixed vaguely upon her, lent such unusual vigor to her limbs that her mallet head straightened, the ball ran true, and a challenged Lance began to mutter, "What the hell?"

"Well, now, how can I help you?" Henry Stockbridge said briskly, taking a seat.

Sergeant Putnam plunged right in.

"You've been noticed observing the moccasin shop on Route 117 where the Blossoms of God are now living."

Henry stared into middistance. A flush spread up his neck and suffused his face. "Oh my Lord. Someone spotted me, did they?"

"I'm afraid they did, sir. I was told by the young people who live there that you've been watching them from the woods."

"Oh my Lord," said Henry again. "What can I say? I can't deny it, but how to explain? I'm a man of action, you see, thirty years of active duty and now I'm old issue. Takes time to adjust. I have my hobbies, my model tanks, my patch collection, but hobbies are hobbies, don't take the place of action. You understand that, don't you, Sergeant? I came up here about a month ago to help my aunt open up the place and I saw this bunch prancing around the lawn and I couldn't figure out what they wanted, couldn't figure out their relationship to my aunt. So I said to myself, Henry, here's a task for you. Get out in the field and reconnoiter. So I ran a few patrols, wrote up my notes, gave myself a full report. But to think that they spotted me," he said sadly. "I slipped up somewhere, slipped up badly. My God, I could have been shot or taken prisoner!"

"We're not at war, sir," Sergeant Putnam reminded him. "The Blossoms are just a bunch of kids."

"They're either that or deucedly clever."

"Have you found any evidence of illegal activity? Any evidence of sinister connections? Any evidence that they meant to harm your aunt?"

"I haven't come up with anything yet," Henry admitted reluctantly. "Of course I've had limited access to written records."

"How have you had access to *any* written records?"

"That's classified information."

"You mean you went into the cabin when they weren't there?"

"They never lock the door," Henry admitted. "By God, I wonder how they spotted me. By God, that's a hard thing to accept, that stings, that does, to an old soldier, to find that he's failed in the field."

"Well, sir, I wouldn't take it too much to heart. As you say, you were working under difficult conditions. Probably just by chance that you were seen at all."

"Don't spare me, Sergeant. My days in the field are over. I won't march again until that last great review before the Five-Star General."

And he jerked his head heavenward, causing Ted to gaze innocently upward as though expecting an apparition to come floating over the chimney.

From the lawn came the steady thwack, thwack of wood against wood and muttered curses from a routed Lance.

"That girl's got a heft to her," Ted observed.

"My daughter, sir," Henry Stockbridge said complacently. "An army brat, that's Mary Lou. Traipsed from one end of the world to the other with her daddy and proud to do it."

"Colonel Stockbridge," Sergeant Putnam said, recalling him to the task at hand, "you didn't happen to reconnoiter last Friday, did you?"

"I believe I did. We came up Thursday evening, Ellen and I, to lend a hand. Did some errands Friday morning, did some reading, had lunch, nipped over for a look-see at fifteen hundred hours while the subjects were cavorting on the lawn."

"Did you go by the clothesline?"

"Yes, sir. Approached from the rear."

"Think carefully about that clothesline, Colonel, and try to remember if the whole line was full of those yellow robes they wear or if there was a gap at one end."

"I see a gap. Wouldn't swear to it in a court of law, if

that's what you're after. Not a bad subterfuge, wearing a robe. That's what you think the murderer did, is it?"

"Yes, we do."

"Think I might have come up with the idea, do you? I take that as a compliment. I wouldn't have put that robe back on the line though. More sensible to take one from inside and return to same."

"They have extra robes inside?"

"Cupboard to the left of the chimney, bottom shelf. Second drawback to me as a suspect, I had no reason or desire to kill my aunt."

"I hate to mention it, sir, but there is the inheritance. That often proves to be reason enough."

"Ah well, I don't doubt it. But what I want, gentlemen, money can't buy: to be eighteen years old again and looking that recruiting sergeant right in the eye."

Ten minutes later the two men left Pineacres, having made their exit through the kitchen where they conversed briefly with Mrs. Stroud, who was white to the elbows with flour and predictably prickly at the interruption.

"Mrs. Turnbull says Paul was the child of the daughter of very close friends of her aunt and uncle," Sergeant Putnam told her, in answer to which Mrs. Stroud violently slapped down a smooth mound of dough on a floured bread board. "These friends couldn't keep the baby after his parents were killed because the wife was dying of cancer. So they gave him to a couple over fifty?"

"You think there's something funny about that? Don't you know these old families? They're like a club. They knew that Paul would get his dues paid with the Stockbridges; that was the important thing, not how old they were."

"You wouldn't know the name of this couple?"

"No, I would not. Now, if you'll excuse me, I have work to do."

And picking up a cinnamon shaker she liberally dusted both the rolled dough and the front of Sergeant Putnam's trousers.

"We're going to Dogtown," Sergeant Putnam told Ted as they rolled down the driveway.

"Why?" Ted wondered, lost in a dreamy perusal of the gardens.

"Something Mrs. Turnbull said about Paul being as dark as a Stroud."

"She meant it as a joke."

"But there is a resemblance, Ted, and it's not just the coloring. I want to meet some more Strouds."

"Okay by me," Ted agreed amiably, "as long as I don't miss my lunch."

chapter TWELVE

Dogtown consisted of an area of poverty-level housing spread on both sides of Route 117 about a mile beyond the lake. Dwellings were placed haphazardly on plots of hard-packed earth fronting a network of unpaved roads. Exterior decor fell within the general category of shabby; some buildings displayed peeling paint, others weathered boards; some were covered with tarpaper in varying degrees of shredding, and there were a large number of permanently settled mobile homes with tipping porches and dangling trim. The yards were choked with a monumental display of rusting car bodies, old refrigerators, and stained mattresses. Sergeant Putnam was glad, for Bea's sake, to see a large number of dogs lunging on chains or leaping forward to raise a deafening alarm. They seemed to be all of one breed, a lean, scruffy, frantic breed with faces like coyotes.

"Stop here," Ted commanded, when they had passed three consecutive mailboxes labeled with the surname Stroud. "I'll ask directions at the next house."

And as Sergeant Putnam watched in awed admiration, Ted calmly opened the door and slid out into the midst of the milling pack.

"Now see here, boys," Sergeant Putnam heard him say, "I'm looking for Estelle Stroud's house."

He came back to direct Sergeant Putnam down the first road to the left, the cruiser swinging through the potholes, many of them still brimming with yesterday's rain. Solemn little children appeared to grow from the soil like mushrooms; round-faced and black-eyed, in dirty jeans and scraps of dresses, they stared at the invading vehicle.

"Third house on the right," said Ted, shaking his head mournfully at the sight of these tiny products of self-indulgence.

They pulled up before a small cottage which was distinguished from its neighbors by the relative magnificence of its yard. Pink flagstones led past an ancient lilac bush which straggled skyward, buttressed with stout poles and bound with twine, and in whose shadow a deck chair sat like a throne. In the center of the patch of worn earth to the left of the path stood a plastic column topped with a silver reflecting globe and at the foot of this ornament a group of plaster elves was diligently raking, hoeing, and shoveling. Under the front windows lay two narrow flower beds in which someone had planted crooked rows of marigolds.

Ted admired the elves, coveted the flagstones, and recommended an application of lime to the lilac. Dirty net curtains stirred at one of the windows in answer to Sergeant Putnam's knock, which also brought a member of the wolf pack thundering around the corner of the house. In response to Ted's crooning the animal dropped to a crouch and wriggled forward on its belly, whining, to rub his muzzle on Ted's shoes.

"Low self-esteem," said Ted sadly.

The woman who opened the door was as dark as Mrs. Stroud but heavy in body, with a puffy face that spoke of ill-health. Long strands of gray hair hung uncombed to her shoulders. She was wearing a faded housedress, a cardigan, and bedroom slippers and she peered at them listlessly through the half-opened door. Sergeant Putnam explained that, as part of the investigation into Mrs.

Stockbridge's death, they were seeking information from anyone who had known her, however remotely. As an old family retainer, he was hoping she could be of some help.

"I guess you've got me mixed up with my sister. I'm Noreen. Come in if you want to. I can't stand up for long."

Waving them through the doorway, she sank heavily into a rocker next to which stood a canister of oxygen.

"We're looking for someone who remembers events twenty-five or thirty years ago," Sergeant Putnam told her. "I know that your mother was working at Pineacres about that time."

"Oh yes, Ma worked up there," Noreen told them apathetically, her energies devoted to respiration. "Estelle started young, too. I was never that much involved except for the heavy cleaning every spring. Thirty years ago you want? You ought to talk to Grandma. She knows a lot about Pineacres."

"I didn't know she was still alive."

"She's right in the next room. She stays in bed until afternoons. Go ahead in. There's nothing wrong with her but being ninety-six years old. She loves a visitor."

The two men entered a tiny hallway that led out of the kitchen.

"On the left," Noreen called after them and they dutifully turned in that direction to find themselves in a small bedroom whose windows overlooked a dump. The room was sparsely furnished with a cluttered bureau and a straight wooden chair and dominated by a tarnished brass bed in which a tiny figure sat propped up against a heap of pillows, her eyes, as dark as prunes, gleaming in a shrunken sparrow's face, skin pulled tightly over beaky nose and high cheekbones. Bare scalp shone pink between thin strands of white hair which had been gathered into a ball and twisted up with a comb on the top of her head. She was wrapped in a crocheted shawl wound over a gray cardigan over a woolen knitted vest over a flannel nightgown, and she stared at them appraisingly from her nest of pillows, then burst into a toothless grin.

"Lost your way, have you?"

"We're investigating . . ."

"Sit down," the old lady commanded them imperiously. Her voice was stronger than Sergeant Putnam had expected from such a diminutive frame, deep and rather hoarse.

"One of you will have to sit on the bed. They've taken away all my chairs."

Ted immediately dropped into the proffered seat, leaving Sergeant Putnam no option but to plant his buttocks gingerly on an ancient stained quilt.

"So you are investigating, are you?" she mocked him. "Investigating old ladies in their bedrooms?"

"Investigating the death of Eunice Stockbridge. We're talking to people who knew her, past or present, and your granddaughter told us that you worked for many years at Pineacres."

"I'm surprised she got that straight. She hasn't a brain in her head. Yes, I worked at Pineacres. Started at fifteen, before I knew better. That was in 1902, the year Francis was born. I knew them all, Francis, Winthrop, Edith, Harold, and George. I can tell you anything you want to know. Edith died young, so did Harold. Francis was a charming crook, Winthrop wore woollen underwear, George was a moron. Got himself blown up before anyone found out."

"Ah, it's the next generation we're most interested in. You must have been there when they were children."

"Louise, you mean? Little Goody Two-Shoes, I used to call *her*. Pity money doesn't buy looks, isn't it? Her brother trailed behind her without a thought of his own and Avery's mother was a slut."

"How about Paul?"

"I didn't know Paul. I retired in 1952."

"I see. And Paul was born in 1955."

"Was he? I wouldn't know."

"Your daughter was working up there then?"

"That's right."

"You knew Paul was adopted?"

"Everyone knew it. Eunice Stockbridge was over fifty years old and looked it."

"Well, thank you, Mrs. Stroud."

"It's Belknap," the old lady snapped. "Augusta Belknap. Can't you even get a name straight? Some investigators you are," she continued with her mirthless grin. "Who let you in here anyway? I have no control over my life anymore. No control over my life or my house."

"This is your house?"

"Of course it's my house. Who told you it wasn't? Did you think it was Estelle's? Estelle could live with her daughter but she'd rather live with me; Annie's husband is an idiot. My daughter, Blanche, lived with me because she was sick and her husband died years ago in a logging accident, head was crushed like an eggshell. Noreen is a charity case but I can't put her out in the cold. They like to pretend they're taking care of me, she and Estelle. I'll outlive them both."

"Your granddaughters aren't married?"

"That's a good question. You'd wonder, wouldn't you, who would marry a retarded girl. But people do. Noreen's had three husbands. They all left her. I wasn't surprised. Estelle's husband has been in Walpole for eighteen years. Did well, didn't they?"

"Ah, thanks again, Mrs. Belknap."

"Yes, hurry away," she said grimly, as Sergeant Putnam eased himself off the bed. "You've brightened my morning considerable. Thank you so very much for dropping in."

"Goodness," murmured Ted as they retraced their way down the hall. Noreen was seated where they had left her, staring at the grease-stained walls of her diminished world whose yellowed sink and battered appliances spoke so eloquently of deprivation. Sergeant Putnam thought of the gleaming modern kitchen at Pineacres and achieved a certain sympathy with Estelle Stroud's grimness.

"Sometimes Grandma's helpful, sometimes she's not," Noreen told them, without turning her head. "You ought to talk to my sister. She's the one that works at Pineacres."

The dog was asleep in the shade of the lilacs and rolled over lazily to watch them depart, growling halfheartedly. Several small boys who had been exploring the cruiser's taillights with gentle fingers, stepped quickly to the opposite side of the road and reacted with studied blankness to Sergeant Putnam's greeting.

The two men sat wrapped in thought as the cruiser threaded its way back through the maze of muddy lanes to the highway. They were passing the outskirts of Hampford Center before either spoke.

"If Noreen is retarded," Ted announced, "so am I," a statement to which Sergeant Putnam could find no possible rejoinder.

He retaliated instead with the results of his own cogitation.

"Ted," he said, "I want you to go over to Mount Pleasant and look through the county birth records and find out how many male babies were born on or near Paul's date of birth, March 13, 1955. Take it at least a month on either side."

"What are you thinking, Dave? He wasn't born out here."

"I'm thinking there must be a reason for the old lady to lie. And don't tell me she got confused; she's as sharp as a tack. It was a deliberate lie, Ted; she didn't want us to know that she was at Pineacres when Paul was adopted. Doesn't that point to some connection between herself and the event? People make a bundle of money out of under-the-counter adoptions. I'm wondering if that's what Mrs. Belknap did; she was up there, she knew how intensely they longed for a baby. Say she also knew of a young girl in trouble. She could have made a tidy pile."

"Well, that's true," Ted conceded. "And I can see her doing it, too, Dave. I bet she'd sell her own mother."

They found Chief Henderson in his office hunched over a cup of lukewarm coffee and a couple of Hostess crumb cakes. He was not particularly enthusiastic about sending Ted to Mount Pleasant.

"It seems to me, Dave, you're going off at a tangent. You may prove the old lady arranged the adoption but what has that got to do with the case at hand?"

"Just as much as the Blossoms missing a robe. The truth is, Len, we don't know at this stage what information is relevant and what isn't. This is a hazy area. Sometimes behind the haze the sun is shining."

"And sometimes it's snowing. Now, I don't think anyone expects us to have the case solved *today*. I mean, we haven't even had the inquest yet! On the other hand, Walfield and Myron are full of good advice and I had a call from the D.A.'s office this morning, just 'keeping in touch.' It all adds up. What I'm trying to say, Dave, there are pressures of time, whether we like it or not, and I can't afford to have my staff chasing rainbows."

"If Ted finds something over there," Sergeant Putnam

persisted stubbornly, "we won't have to go through the Boston records."

"Go through the what?" Chief Henderson cried, spraying Hostess crumbs to the four winds. "Did you hear one single word I said? Do you know how much of a job that would be? Who would do that as a favor to me?"

"Me," said Ted, who was waiting patiently in the doorway. "As long as I got my lunch on the way."

"You are not going to Boston," shouted Chief Henderson. "You are going to Mount Pleasant."

"Okay," agreed Ted. "I'll eat at the Primrose. You ever tasted their banana cream pie? Of course the blueberry is scrumptious and they're famous for their apple, but to my way of thinking, the banana . . ."

"Get out of here," Chief Henderson bellowed and Ted, who was often dismissed with these very words, departed with visions of banana cream dancing in his head.

"I count on my staff," Chief Henderson observed gloomily, "to smooth my way, not to throw stones in the path." He took a sip of glacial coffee. "I haven't even mentioned the fact that my stomach is beginning to roil. I didn't want there to be the slightest suspicion that I was making a bid for sympathy and understanding."

"I'm sorry about your stomach, Len."

"Thank you. So am I. I dislike pain. Now tell me again about your morning. Did you see Henry Stockbridge? And what do you think of the likelihood of his being a murderer?"

"He can't be dismissed as a possibility, Len, if only because he was so definitely in the right place at the right time. He was over there Friday afternoon nosing around their cabin while the Blossoms were at Pineacres, and not for the first time either. He had plenty of opportunity to take a robe, do the deed, and put it back. Also, whoever took that robe didn't take it off the line Friday or it would have filled the same space when he put it back, not the empty space. Which makes Henry's statements all the more damning. He admitted that he knew there were extra robes in the house and where they were and that he had been inside their cabin on previous occasions; they don't believe in locking up. Of course, if Henry knew that, someone else could have known it, too. The fact that the Blossoms were absent for a couple of hours every weekday afternoon was common knowledge to everyone at Pineacres. If someone took the robe on Friday, the possibilities extend to a lot of people, and just because Henry didn't mention any names doesn't mean that he couldn't have seen someone else that afternoon and be covering for him. If, on the other hand, the robe was taken before Friday, the field is narrowed to the Strouds and Mary Lou."

"It sounds like a brainteaser," Chief Henderson groaned. "Give me professionals any day to these amateur productions."

"Oh, we have one."

"One what?"

"Professional. Leon Stroud, Mrs. Stroud's husband, professional burglar. He's been in Walpole for eighteen years, according to Grandma."

"No kidding. The skeleton in the closet, eh?"

"Might be worthwhile checking him out."

"You think he stretched his arms between the bars and all the way to Hampford?"

"Obviously he didn't do it himself, Len. But how do we know he didn't influence someone else. His son, for instance . . ."

"Well, yes," Chief Henderson conceded, bringing to mind Wayne's shifty-eyed, glowering visage. "I'll give you that, Dave. I'll see what I can dig up on Leon Stroud, who visits him, et cetera. In return for which . . ."

"I knew it."

". . . in return for the hefty concessions I have made to you in the last ten minutes, I expect you to play local policeman for the afternoon. These big cases tend to go to your head; you get locked on to one like a bird dog on a scent. But we've still got a town to serve."

"Yes, Len."

"Furthermore, I think it would be expedient on our part to ease up on the Stockbridges temporarily. I have a feeling they're going to have their hands full with the press this afternoon. I've already given my 'no comment' three times this morning, so somebody's onto the story. And you know our men of the media if they sense any attempted suppression of facts. Mrs. Turnbull will be wise to get off her high horse. Oh, Dave," he added with a grimace, as Sergeant Putnam rose, "if you go out for lunch will you get me some Tums?"

chapter THIRTEEN

Sergeant Putnam plodded dutifully through his afternoon, picking away at the remains of yesterday's paperwork and soothing an irate Pennsylvania tourist whose Lincoln Continental received a gruesome scrape outside the Olde Chestnut Gifte Shoppe. He recovered an independent four-year-old from an unauthorized stroll, and was back in time to run the town's handyman, Emery Gould, to the Mount Pleasant hospital after he had inexplicably entangled an electric hedge clipper in his iron-gray curls, sustaining some superficial but messy scalp lacerations.

"Why, the goddamn thing just took right off," he told Sergeant Putnam, spraying spittle in his excitement, head wrapped in gauze from the station's first aid kit. "Turned on me like a wild beast."

Sergeant Putnam returned to an hour's hard labor, working out the details of the police department's annual bicycle inspection and gymkhana. And all the while one part of his mind was following Ted bite by bite through his banana cream pie and step by step up the granite stairs to the courthouse. As the minutes ticked by and the hours passed, a new image sprang to mind, of Ted trapped beneath his overturned car in some inaccessible gully. There was simply no other explanation for such a delay. Nobody, not even Ted, could take so long to come up with a few bits of routine information.

119

The little hand stood on the five and the big hand on the ten before he picked up Ted's wheezy approach, appended by a short delay on the top step while he caught his breath and fumbled with the door handle.

Sergeant Putnam with great effort restrained the words that were on his tongue. The slightest sign of disapproval was enough to bring forth fifteen minutes of rambling justification; the slightest hint of impatience would drive Ted into a further fifteen minutes of old-maidish fussing.

"Well," he said with a stretch, exaggerating the casual, "what did you find out?"

But his question was premature. Ted was still preparing himself, unbuttoning his jacket, aligning his cap on the table, tugging in turn each trouser leg to relieve the strain upon the crease of a sitting position. A little flick at a speck of piecrust on his right sleeve, a glance at his fingernails, and he was ready to commence.

"Gee, I had a funny afternoon," he said, taking a moment to relish the memory. "Came out of the Primrose and ran smack into Bea Lambert, of all people. She was over there on the senior citizens' bus, doing her bit of shopping. Well, we chatted for a minute or two and then I went on my way to the courthouse where I did what you wanted me to do which took longer than I thought it would so that I came out just about snack time. So being but two streets away, it seemed a crying shame not to nip back to the Primrose and try the rhubarb-strawberry, which came mighty close to my Aunt Clara's except that she added a handful of raisins and I don't know but that they did point up the taste. But raisins or no, it went down easy and I had a cup of coffee, but only the one because of having to get back here to report and knowing you were going to be all excited when I told you what I found out."

"Wha . . ."

"*Just* as I reached my car," Ted said, shaking his head in amazement, "there she was again, Bea Lambert, smack dab in front of me. Now wasn't that some coincidence?"

"It sure was. Did you tell her why you were over there?"

"Just enough to settle her curiosity. I know how much to give a woman like Bea."

Sergeant Putnam groaned inwardly. Ted was no match for Bea even at less than her subtle best. He had no doubt that she had milked Ted dry.

"Well, she was finished with her little purchases and it seemed a neighborly thing to offer her a ride in my vehicle which was parked right beside us, but then of course we had to go searching for Tessie Eaton and the senior citizens' bus so they wouldn't think Bea had run away or been taken ill or been mugged," added Ted, conscientiously running the gamut of possibilities, "lying in an alley with her little beaded purse emptied out. Well, sir, after some circling around we found the bus parked where it ought to be but not a soul in it, and I guess it was about twenty minutes before the seniors began to file back and we could leave a message for Tessie which we did and then we headed for home. . . ."

Sergeant Putnam fought down an impulse to scream.

"Let's put it into fast-forward, Ted. You and Bea are having a nice chat on the way to Hampford . . . now you're pulling into her driveway next to her famous climbing rose . . . now it's goodbye Bea and here you are. What did you find out in Mount Pleasant?"

A hurt expression crossed Ted's seamed face and for a moment he teetered on the edge of a sulk, but the desire to impart his information won out over resentment.

"I found out something very interesting, Dave. You gave me the date, March the thirteenth, nineteen hundred and fifty-five. Two girls born on that date, no boys, so I started working my way forward for a week and then back for a week and then I took the next week on either end. See, that's the way I do it, Dave; that's my method. Work forward and work back. So we come to March the fourth, nineteen hundred and fifty-five and what do you suppose I found? A male child," said Ted, spacing his words for emphasis, "a male child born to Noreen Stroud of Sheffield Township."

"Well, I'll be damned. Somehow I'm not too surprised, are you, Ted? The old lady knew a girl in trouble all right."

"She was only fifteen," Ted said sadly. "Noreen, I mean, not the old lady."

"Fifteen in nineteen fifty-five . . . why, that makes her only forty-three years old, Ted. I would have guessed ten years older. I thought she was Mrs. Stroud's elder sister. But Mrs. Stroud," he said, fishing through the papers on his desk for his notebook and turning to a scribbled page, "Mrs. Stroud is forty-eight so she's the elder sister. She was already married when Noreen had the baby. It *must* have been Paul. It's too damn much of a coincidence for anything else. Proving it will be another matter. I doubt if we have enough of a case to convince a judge to unseal Paul's original birth certificate. It requires a damn strong reason and I have to agree with Len, I don't see how we can tie this in with Eunice Stockbridge's death."

"Where *is* Len?"

"He went home early. His stomach's upset. Walfield called about an hour ago with some helpful hints for running a homicide investigation. Seems everything he mentioned was something Len hadn't done."

"Poor Len," Ted commiserated comfortably, as one who had eschewed responsibility and its headaches. He glanced up at the clock with a practiced motion and found that, as he had expected, it was suppertime.

Returning refreshed an hour later, he relieved Sergeant Putnam, who had made two phone calls in his absence, the first, despite Len's admonition, to Pineacres; he was anxious to talk to Paul directly, but Paul, Louise Turnbull informed him coldly, had not returned. When and if he did return, he would receive Sergeant Putnam's message. His second call was likewise greeted curtly, as Chief Henderson was awaiting word from the warden's office at Walpole regarding Leon Stroud and the call had assumed exaggerated importance as a means of assuaging his guilt at deserting the office prematurely. His aching stomach and a vision of conceivable future unemployment were absorbing his attention to such a degree that he showed little interest in Sergeant Putnam's revelation, although he did not close the door entirely on the desirability and possibility of obtaining Paul's birth certificate.

It was Sergeant Putnam who had now lost much of his original zest at pursuing this particular line of inquiry, but he was methodical by nature and with the aim of finishing what he had started, he instructed Ted to have Paul call him at home if Paul should try to reach him that evening. Ted inscribed the message in his loopy handwriting on the memo pad that was the sole object on his desk, and leaving him absorbed in the latest edition of the Salvation Army's *War Cry,* Sergeant Putnam trudged home through the evening shadows in the perfumed air of a late spring day.

With only one week remaining in the school year, parents were already slackening their grip; the smell of charcoal fires drifted from more than one backyard and the sidewalk was congested with youngsters on bicycles and roller skates. His own boys were playing a spirited game of basketball beneath a hoop mounted above the garage door. Tom, at twelve, was still a child, but Davey, two years older, had begun a metamorphosis that had taken his father by surprise. Where had he come from, this raucous young stranger? How could those gigantic hands belong to Davey, the corded forearms, the fierce new masculinity that was both delight and threat? Davey tossed him the ball as he approached, a hard pass that he nearly fumbled; he tried a looping outside shot and missed. Why did he read challenge into every act between them? What did he fear? Mockery in Davey's eyes replacing the admiration?

The boys trailed him into the house; he was a source of information with which to impress classmates and he had to be careful how much he said in front of them.

Barbara, removing a steaming chicken pie from the oven, said, "I'm glad you're late because I am, too. I had a visitor. Someone who's very fond of you, Dave." She laughed. "I wonder if I ought to be jealous."

Sergeant Putnam removed his jacket and washed his hands at the sink. Jenny was already in her chair, tapping tunes with her fork on her milk glass and humming violently.

"It can't be Bea," Sergeant Putnam said, taking his place. "She spent the afternoon in Mount Pleasant."

"No, it wasn't Bea. Jenny, stop that, please, honey, I'm trying to talk to Daddy. Dave, why don't you serve the pie while I dish out the coleslaw.

"I was downtown," Barbara said, "doing a few errands after school when I saw this little fat person carrying a bag of groceries from Randall's and I knew who she was, of course, as I'd seen her with old Mrs. Stockbridge on a number of occasions, so I went up and said hello. I'm not quite sure why, but she looked so alone somehow. I don't know who she thought I was, a reporter perhaps, she looked so startled, and when I introduced myself, thinking to reassure her, for goodness' sake, Dave, she dropped the whole bag of groceries. Just let it go. I've never seen anyone do that before except in cartoons. Well, anyway, I helped her pick things up and then we got onto the subject of you. I didn't realize I was married to such a paragon of virtue."

The boys were grinning at his discomposure.

"We saw her." Tom laughed. "Ma brought her home."

"Yes, I did," Barbara admitted. "She just stood there, Dave, in those god-awful shorts. I had to do something and I'm glad I did because she's really a nice little person and I enjoyed getting to know her."

"We had lemonade and we had cookies," Jenny informed him, anxious to supplement the tale. "Mary Lou ate a lot of cookies."

"She just seems to munch along without being aware of what she's doing," Barbara mused.

"What did you talk about? Besides me."

"Well, let me see. Mostly, I think about her inheritance. She found out yesterday that she's getting a lot of money and it seems very worrisome to her, the feeling that she has to do something with it and not knowing what to do and afraid she'll do the wrong thing. I told her I had read somewhere that the way to find out what you really want to do is to think back over your life and pick out the times when you've been the happiest and try to find the common denominator. So she thought and she thought and then she remembered this old cocker spaniel that her family had for years who used to sleep all the time and what made her happy was lying next to the dog on a rug or on the grass and listening to it breathe."

"The dog's name was Bimbo," said Jenny. "I don't

think that's a nice name for a dog. I would never call my dog Bimbo."

"Mary Lou is a realist," said her father.

"Another thing that made her happy was saying good-bye. Her father was an army officer, you see, which meant frequent moves and she was never happier than when she was leaving, which is perfectly understandable when you consider what kind of school experiences she must have had. Maybe every move carried the hope of something different."

"I'd call it Blackie or Woofie," Jenny insisted, "or Spotty or Whitey."

"The third thing she remembered, Dave, was being happy on the day *after* Christmas, not on Christmas Day like other kids but on the day after the holiday because then she could savor her memories without worrying about anything going wrong to spoil the day."

"So what did you make out of all this?" Sergeant Putnam asked, forking in his pie. "It can't always be the day after Christmas."

"No, I admit I was kind of on the spot, so I said, sort of grabbing at straws, that maybe she should get a dog and travel and she said it would have to be an old ugly dog and I said I thought there were plenty of those around, and at that she brightened right up and said I'd been a great help to her, although goodness knows how."

*　　　*　　　*

Sergeant Putnam was sitting on the glider on the front porch with a can of beer when Paul Stockbridge called at half-past eight.

Paul agreed ungraciously to talk to Sergeant Putnam but refused his offer to come to Pineacres, preferring to meet him at the station. Ted remained diplomatically concealed behind the counter with the *Mount Pleasant Times* crossword puzzle and Sergeant Putnam ushered Paul toward one of the plastic chairs in the waiting room that looked so unrelievedly shoddy under artificial light. Paul had lost some of his self-assurance; he appeared hot and rumpled and glum. Vangie, it transpired, had not returned with him to Hampford. Her parents, according to Paul, were being incredibly parochial about the murder and she thought it best to stay and pacify them.

"I haven't even eaten," Paul said gloomily. "What's so important?"

"Paul, what do you know about your adoption?"

"My adoption?" Paul asked startled. "What's that got to do with anything?"

"Have you ever tried to trace your biological parents?"

"They died when I was a baby. That's why I was given to Mother and Dad."

"What did your mother tell you about your parents?"

"Why should I tell you what my mother told me about my parents? You haven't told me why you want to know."

"Bear with me, Paul. In the course of an investigation of this type we sift through an enormous amount of information, a lot of which turns out to be completely without relevance to the homicide. But how do we know in advance which line of inquiry is going to prove productive? We don't. So please be patient even though some of my questions seem extraneous to you."

"Hey, okay, if you put it that way. I didn't know you *had* a plan. I thought you were just bumbling along hoping you'd stumble over something. I really don't know a helluva lot about police departments, but they've never impressed me as particularly efficient."

"We do our best," Sergeant Putnam said tritely.

"Hey, of course you do. I mean, don't take it personally or anything. I want to know who killed Mother, too."

"Were you close to her?"

"They were very good to me," Paul said loyally.

"You never felt their age any handicap?"

"Hell, no. They were settled and rich; they thought the sun rose and set on me, more like doting grandparents maybe, but there's lots of kids who do worse than that. My father never raised his voice to me, let alone his hand."

"And your mother?"

"Oh, Mother and I had our moments," Paul admitted, "but I always got around her in the end. Mother was a good sport."

He looked down pensively at his strong brown hands.

"What are you doing about that wacky cult?" he asked with an edge to his voice. "I have all I can do when I drive by that place not to run in there and throttle a confession out of one of those creeps. Now, don't worry," he added quickly, flashing his disarming smile, "I don't do *everything* I want to do."

"Frankly, Paul, the Blossoms of God had very little motive to kill your mother. They gained nothing by her death, whereas a number of other people stand to gain a great deal."

"If you're intimating that my cousins had anything to do with it," Paul told him, eyes narrowing, "you're opening yourself to a lawsuit. Louise *saw* one of those Blossoms going down the stairs, for God's sake. What more do you need?"

"She saw somebody in a yellow robe, Paul."

"Well, hell, I don't want to argue. I guess Wayne Stroud's a better bet anyway."

"You think he'd kill your mother for a Buick?"

"He'd kill for a buck. He's put me against the wall a

few times. There were a couple of scrapes I got into in my teens that I didn't want Mother and Dad to know about, nothing more than any normal kid gets into, but still it might have been a little sticky and Wayne, hell, he helped me out the one time and then turned around and blackmailed me, the sneaky bastard."

"Are you saying he demanded money from you to keep quiet?"

"Demanded and got it. Of course, I got a little older and told him to go to hell. But for a couple of years, he did pretty well. That's the kind of person he is."

"I see."

"Yeah, well, what was your question anyway?"

"I think I asked you what you were told about your biological parents."

"Well, Mother explained to me that they had these friends who had a married daughter and she and her husband had a baby boy, which was me, and one night my parents went out to a party and coming home this drunk kid smashed into their car and killed them. I was only a couple of months old so obviously I don't remember anything about them. My grandparents knew they wouldn't be able to take care of me because my grandmother was dying of cancer and they thought of Mother and Dad and that's how it went."

"What was their name?"

"I don't know my grandparents' name. My parents' name was Richardson, Nancy and Benjamin Richardson. I was Paul James, but Mother and Dad changed it to Paul Winthrop after Dad."

"Did they live in Boston?"

"I don't know where they lived. My grandparents lived in Boston but I don't know if my parents did. I've just never had a helluva lot of interest in any of them.

What was the point? They were all dead and I was perfectly happy where I was."

"Yes, of course. Well, thank you very much, Paul," Sergeant Putnam said, rising. "I know it was a chore to come down here but every bit helps."

"I hope something does," Paul answered, shaking hands at the door and vanishing into the darkness.

Ted's voice rose over the counter like that of a disembodied spirit.

"What's a three-letter word for Balaam's beast?"

chapter FOURTEEN

Mrs. Stroud cornered Louise Turnbull just before dinner Monday evening and told her firmly that no one person could be expected to cook, serve, *and* clean; Annie's varicose veins were bad, her husband, Roy, had totaled their car, little Jimmy had convulsions . . . the upshot being that Mary Lou spent her evening vacuuming the upstairs bedrooms and scrubbing three baths. Cut off from communication by the whine of the machine, she shuffled along in a haze of her own thoughts, sorting out the emotions engendered by the afternoon's adventure. If only Barbara hadn't been so nice. It was impossible, decided Mary Lou, sucking up a dead spider with the upholstery attachment, to hate Barbara. Face it, she told herself gloomily, you've made a friend at the expense of something grander. Take the noble path. Be happy that he's happy.

A late snack of pizza from the freezer consoled her aching heart and she climbed the stairs resigned to interacting with Sergeant Putnam on an intellectual level. Moonlight spilled through her curtainless window and she lay gazing out at the silvery sky and listening to the sounds of the household settling for the night. Uncle Malcolm had arrived; she heard him shout something to Aunt Louise about a water faucet; her parents' bedroom door shut; her mother laughed. Sometime later Lance's Mustang throbbed into the yard. Mary Lou's eyelids dropped and she slipped into sleep.

*　　*　　*

Crack, sounded the second step; she was aware of the origin of the noise before she was fully awake. Creak, crack, the floorboards protested the passage of weight along the hallway. Paul's door snapped shut. Mary Lou rolled over and eyed the luminous dial of her bedside clock. Twelve-fifteen. Goodness, where had he been? Back to see Vangie? Poor Paul. He was too dumb to see that Vangie was even dumber. Something was weighing on her heart. Oh yes, she had made the supreme sacrifice. Never mind "poor Paul." How about poor Mary Lou!

She sighed and twisted in her narrow bed but sleep eluded her. Nothing for it; there was only one cure. Clambering out of bed she pulled on her bathrobe and padded barefoot into the hall. Indistinct muffled sounds were coming from behind Paul's door. Pressing her ear to the panel, Mary Lou was amazed to identify the gasps of distressed sobbing. She had never heard Paul cry before, not even as a little boy; Aunt Eunice would be gratified to have produced such desolation. Or was a more realistic source of grief his relationship with Vangie? Was the situation blacker than anyone had guessed? In which case, thought Mary Lou, tiptoeing quickly away along the hall and down the stairs, avoiding the second step, in which case, she bore the responsibility for Paul's condition, she and her headlong crusade for justice. Paul's life had been a sunny meadow; she ought to have known he couldn't handle clouds. Grief and heartache had to be practiced from the beginning, like playing scales.

Halfway down the third-floor stairway her foot encountered something smooth and slippery and cold; for a horrible moment she thought she had stepped on a slug. The experience lent caution to the remainder of the journey, but without further incident she reached the kitchen and snapped on the overhead light. Mrs. Stroud's glossy linoleum was marred by several gray streaks, and by the doormat a dark blob that proved to be a lump of mud in a strange shape. Picking it up and studying it, Mary Lou realized that it conformed to a piece of the pattern on the sole of a sneaker. Paul had been walking in the mud; it had to have been Paul to have left a similar piece on the third-floor stairway. This was lakeshore mud; she recognized the smell, the color, the consistency. The information clicked into her mind and instantaneously came the readout. "Oh no," said Mary Lou. He hadn't. He hadn't been so overcome that he had actually contemplated wading out into that dark water! She had a terrible image of Paul standing alone with his grief among the tussocks. It was a sobered Mary Lou who cleaned out the cookie jar.

She woke early, despite her troubled night, with sunlight warm on her blanket. The window appeared as a painted backdrop of improbably brilliant blue across which puffy fair-weather clouds made a fleeting visitation. Mary Lou tossed back her covers and arose. She inevitably awoke with a sense of foreboding, or, to be more precise, a feeling of depression assailed her at the realization that she was once more awake. The sole antidote was immediate activity. She pulled on a pair of red stretch slacks and a white T-shirt that ringed her breasts with a circle of grinning multihued faces and the slogan *It's a Small World,* stuck her feet in her sandals and went down the hall to the bathroom to splash cold water on her face and run a comb through her hair. Silence from Paul's room, silence on the second floor, the kitchen empty; Mrs. Stroud arrived at eight.

Mary Lou made herself a cup of tea and four slices of cinnamon toast which she ate at the kitchen table, after which she rinsed her dish and cup neatly at the sink and, wetting a paper towel, wiped the traces of mud from the floor. Through the back window she saw Wayne sally forth from the garage to bend over the gas tank of the power mower. Graunty never let Wayne mow until the grass was dry, that particular contest being only one of numerous continuing skirmishes from which Wayne had now emerged triumphant. No skin off my nose, thought Mary Lou. Let him mow in a snowstorm, if it gratifies his feeble ego.

Intent on enjoying this pristine morning, she went out through the front door and crossed the terrace and the lawn, leaving silver traces in the dew-soaked grass. The lake surface, ruffled by the same wind that was hustling the clouds along, twinkled and glinted with a beauty that belied its muddy depths. With the sunlight warm on her face, Mary Lou squinted at the glittering vista. Birds were singing in the woods, ducks quacking vehemently among the reeds. Her eye was caught by a white object bobbing in the water along the western shore, more the shape of a giant jellyfish than a duck. Whatever the thing might be, it was moving with the wind and the waves straight toward the beach of Pineacres, and since there had never been a giant jellyfish sighted in Lake Wickiwitchi, Mary Lou felt a certain scientific responsibility to study the specimen more closely. She went down to the beach and from there to the end of the dock where she waited expectantly, revising her identification downward from jellyfish to boat cushion.

Then, as the next few feet were covered at the same mincing, bobbing pace, she experienced a nauseating sensation of déjà vu. Was this going to be the story of her life, discovering dead bodies? Had she stumbled on her vocation? This kind of thing didn't happen to other people she knew. Was being the chosen one a sign of favor or disgust? She felt a little sick gazing down on a back in a white T-shirt. Arms and legs lolled underwater and a bald head was riding like a little island, waves washing over it rhythmically. The body floated up against the pilings of the dock and there it held, still bobbing peacefully up and down but no longer making forward progress.

Mary Lou turned and stumbled toward the house and saw to her immense relief her father with his walking stick coming across the lawn. Since his exposure by the Blossoms of God, Henry had done his strolling in the opposite direction, to the end of the lake and back. In good spirits, breathing deeply of the fresh morning air, he raised his stick in greeting to Mary Lou, pleased to see her out so early. With the sun in his eyes, her distress was not evident until they stood toe to toe, so that he was inappropriately cheerful when she blurted out her grim news.

Hurrying back before her to the dock, Henry insisted on standing guard above the body, fearful that some early-rising innocent should venture upon this traumatizing scene. As far as Mary Lou could remember no child at any hour of any day had ever approached the Pineacres beach, but she acquiesced in his concern and trudged toward the house to make the necessary phone call, praying that its occupants were still asleep, thus sparing her the experience of another emotional brouhaha. Lady Luck saw fit to award her one brief passing swipe; she heard movement upstairs, but no curious faces appeared to question her action and from the kitchen came no clink of crockery. An advancing and receding drone beyond the sun porch placed Wayne on the side lawn, insulated from happenings at the lake by a line of shrubbery and the noise of the mower, just retribution, decided Mary Lou, for racketing along at the crack of dawn.

The Hampford police station was not officially manned between the hours of eleven P.M. and eight in the morning, although Chief Henderson was very often at his desk by six-thirty or seven, having run out of chores at home. But even had Mary Lou realized this, she could not, seeking comfort, have leafed through the phone book for any other number than the one she quickly found and dialed. Barbara's cheerful hello caused a moment's disorientation, but she blurted out her message and Barbara hurried to rouse her husband, momentarily reviving Mary Lou's pain with an image of double-bed coziness, although such an arrangement, considered objectively, had always repelled her. She would not have minded sharing her bed with a dog but to have another human body there was a breach of her privacy that appalled her, even in the abstract.

Sergeant Putnam's voice returned her to the problem at hand. His startled reaction to her announcement made him realize that he, like Chief Henderson, had never given full credence to her tale of a T-shirted observer. But Len had gone a step beyond as he found when he called the station.

"My God," Len said. "Leon Stroud."

"What?"

"Leon Stroud, Dave. I got the call last night, didn't seem pressing enough to disturb you. Leon Stroud was released from Walpole two weeks ago and the description fits like a glove: short, heavy, balding, middle-aged. What will you bet it's Leon Stroud?"

"I won't bet anything," said Sergeant Putnam. "You're describing half the male population of Hampford."

chapter FIFTEEN

The new case was incisively appropriated by Lieutenant Walfield. The locals might have achieved control of the first investigation through a deplorable lapse of professionalism but the Stockbridges' idiosyncrasies were not endowed with unlimited influence. Back in his own element, Walfield made his usual efficient, practiced response and Sergeant Putnam and Chief Henderson found themselves standing with Mary Lou and her father, relegated to the role of bystanders. Chief Henderson made his one contribution when he mentioned the name Leon Stroud and saw Walfield's interest quicken. ("My God," said Henry, "I'd almost forgotten she *had* a husband.") But once the information belonged to Walfield, Chief Henderson took a back seat to Mary Lou, who twice, with little prodding, supplied a graphic narration of her discovery.

Sergeant Putnam was dispatched to the house to find Mrs. Stroud and escort her to the scene. An ambulance roared up as he reached the lawn, followed by the lab van, and the growing noise and congestion brought Louise Turnbull onto the terrace, shading her eyes against the sun.

"What in the world is the matter now, Sergeant?" she demanded sharply as he climbed the terrace steps. Malcolm appeared in the doorway behind her dressed in black trousers and a black short-sleeved shirt with clerical collar. Sergeant Putnam realized with a jolt that the inquest into Eunice Stockbridge's death was scheduled to begin in less than an hour.

"What's happening now?"

"I'm afraid there's been a drowning."

"A child?" asked Malcolm fearfully.

"No, sir, a middle-aged man. It's possible that he's Mrs. Stroud's husband. I've come to fetch her."

"But he's in prison."

"He was released two weeks ago. If you'll excuse me, please, sir," and he sidestepped Malcolm and went down the hallway, leaving the Turnbulls transfixed in their surprise.

Mrs. Stroud, caught in the act of tying on her apron, cast upon him her usual disapproving gaze.

"Hard to get breakfast with a kitchen full of people," she observed sourly.

"Never mind breakfast, Mrs. Stroud," Louise said shakily, following Sergeant Putnam into the room. "There's been an accident at the lake."

Mrs. Stroud's face went gray.

"Wayne?" she whispered.

"No, ma'am. But perhaps your husband, Leon Stroud."

"My husband?" she said, looking truly startled. "Is he dead?"

"Yes, ma'am, I'm afraid he is."

"Drowned?"

"It looks that way."

"Well, if that isn't true to form," she said tartly, "to go to all the trouble of escaping and then fall in a lake."

"He didn't escape. He was released two weeks ago."

"Was he?" She measured coffee into a percolator. "You're right in the way of the stove."

"I'm afraid I'll have to ask you to come down and make the identification."

"I haven't seen him for fifteen years."

"Would you rather I ask Wayne to do it?"

"You leave Wayne out of this. Wayne was eight years old when his father went to Walpole. It was a terrible shock to him and I'll not have it all stirred up again. Mrs. Turnbull, that coffee will start to perk in about five minutes, if you don't mind eating yesterday's rolls with it."

"Perhaps I ought to come with you," Louise said nervously. "Should we go to the inquest?"

"By all means," Sergeant Putnam assured her. "There's nothing you can do about this."

She dithered behind him to the terrace where Malcolm was still gazing toward the beach. He seemed mesmerized by this latest unnatural death.

"We're going to the inquest," Louise told him. "There's nothing we can do here."

"Dreadful, dreadful," Malcolm muttered, but for whom he did not specify.

Mrs. Stroud walked briskly across the lawn as though taking care of one more housekeeping task. The body had been removed from the water and was lying face upward on a tarpaulin on the shore. The police photographer was packing his equipment; two ambulance attendants lounged against the side of their vehicle waiting for Dr. Rupert to finish his examination.

"Fellow suffered a broken neck," Dr. Rupert said, standing up and brushing sand off his trouser legs. He nodded in recognition to Sergeant Putnam. "There's a massive amount of bruising coming out on the left side of the body."

Lieutenant Walfield moved forward to intercept Mrs. Stroud and lead her to a spot beside the tarpaulin. Mrs. Stroud gazed down at the sodden remains as though she were judging a turkey for the oven.

"He's let himself go," she observed. "He looks terrible."

"Is this your husband, Leon Stroud?"

"It was."

She turned away as though to retreat to her biscuits but was deflected by Lieutenant Walfield and his notebook.

Hasty statements were obtained as well from the Turnbulls before they left for the inquest, which also required the presence of Lieutenant Walfield and Chief Henderson. Mary Lou had been excused from appearing as though she were a small child or mentally incompetent, a written statement furnishing an acceptable substitute for her attendance, but as a protective device the scheme backfired badly. It would have been far less traumatic, it seemed to Sergeant Putnam, to have had to recount the discovery of the infamous pillowcase than to stand over Leon Stroud's bloated corpse and identify him as the man she had seen prowling around Pineacres.

With the transfer of Leon Stroud's body into the ambulance, cruisers dispersed; Sergeant Putnam was sent to interview the remaining members of the family, while three state policemen carried out the same task at the houses and cottages along the rest of the lakefront. It was apparent that Lieutenant Walfield was not going to wait for the results of an autopsy to treat this death as a potential homicide. Sergeant Putnam could not fault his reasoning. It was hard to see how anyone, even as reputedly inept as Leon Stroud, could manage to break his neck while drowning in a mud-bottomed lake.

He was accompanied to the house by Henry and Mary Lou, Henry pondering the situation aloud as they crossed the lawn. He, too, had grasped the implications of Dr. Rupert's revelations.

"Fellow let his guard down, turned his back on the enemy. Even a recruit knows better than that. Sounds harsh to say it, but he got what he deserved."

"He wasn't a soldier, sir."

"Damn right he wasn't a soldier. Wouldn't have lasted a week in my outfit. In there a while, was he?"

"Rupert says at least six hours, judging from the state of development of the bruises."

"Water temperature would be a factor."

"Undoubtedly."

A gruesome conversation under a benign blue sky, the canopy of a perfect June landscape.

Mary Lou trudged behind them in an agony of indecision, every word of their exchange guaranteed to fuel her mental turmoil. So Paul had been down by the lake last night, she told herself, attempting a casual wave of the hand or mental facsimile thereof. So what? Surely the lake was big enough that one could drown and the other brood without stepping over each other. Paul's presence was entirely irrelevant to Leon Stroud's death. Why then didn't she just speak up? Was she afraid she was not going to get a "so what?" from Sergeant Putnam? A tiny garden toad blinked at her from a pot of geraniums as she mounted the terrace steps and she thought with envy of a life without a cerebral cortex.

Wayne Stroud's voice assailed them as they stepped through the front doorway and his anger became more apparent as they neared the kitchen. He was facing his mother across the table and the entrance of three non-combatants did nothing to check his assault.

"I'm not eight years old anymore, Ma. He was my *father.*"

"I did what I thought was best," Mrs. Stroud replied shortly, turning to face her visitors, Wayne glaring across her shoulder.

"You've been here so long you don't know when you're getting kicked in the teeth. Like why didn't no one else tell me? Like the lawn is more important than me? Don't tell Wayne his father is dead or he might cut the lawn all choppy?"

"Rubbish," Henry Stockbridge said curtly. "And mind how you speak to your mother, my boy. A Gold Star mother is a precious vessel and deserving of respect."

Wayne gaped at him in amazement and it occurred to Sergeant Putnam with a silent chuckle that Henry's formidable value system rendered him virtually impervious to attack. Mrs. Stroud, however, was immune to the power of words and Henry's gallant intervention did not dent her armor.

"Your father has been dead to you for eighteen years," she told Wayne coldly. "You might go tell your sister and your aunt and your grandma before someone else gets to them, which would be a lot more useful than ranting and raving in my kitchen."

"So what was he doing here anyway?" Wayne demanded in a less truculent tone. "Did he come to see you?"

"Apparently not," replied his mother dryly. "I never even knew he was out."

"I'll bet Grandma did."

"Did he keep in touch with your grandmother?" Sergeant Putnam inquired casually, but too much policeman showed; his query united the Strouds against a common enemy and put an end to their disclosures.

The gathering took on a more formal aspect. He asked Mary Lou and her father to rouse the remaining members of the household, and sitting down at the table, he opened his notebook and took a ballpoint pen from his breast pocket.

"I won't keep you long, Mr. Stroud, but I would like to know what you were doing last night."

"Just how did my father die?" Wayne replied, eyeing him shrewdly.

"That's what we're trying to find out, isn't it?" replied Sergeant Putnam with a deliberately bland regard which he held until Wayne lowered his gaze.

"You won't get any help from me. I went out."

"Where?"

"Mount Pleasant."

"Could you be a little more specific?"

"I could."

"Wayne," said his mother sharply, "answer his questions or he'll be here all morning."

"I went to Jolly Jack's."

It was the kind of setting in which Sergeant Putnam could easily picture him, draped across the stained, chipped bar airing his grievances.

"What time did you leave?"

"I wasn't watching the clock."

"Roughly."

"Roughly eleven," Wayne said, mimicking his tone. "I didn't see anybody. I went right to bed."

"Nobody on the lake road?"

"Nope."

"What cars were in the yard?"

"Cars? Well, hell, everybody's, I think. Mal had arrived . . ."

"Mr. Malcolm," snapped his mother.

"*Mr.* Malcolm's car," said Wayne, "was in the yard because Paul had put his precious Corvette in his cousin's place and Avery's antique goes next to that. So there was Mal's in the yard and Mary Lou's and Henry's little rattlebox. Wait a minute. I don't remember seeing Lance's junk heap."

"Thank you, Mr. Stroud."

He turned to Wayne's mother, who stood beside the table, hands gripped across her aproned front.

"I was at home and in bed," she told him flatly,

"having done all Annie's work as well as mine with
out no extra help. I told Mrs. Stockbridge yesterday, I
said it's too much for one person, I'll have to call in
Rhonda, that's my cousin, who's come before. 'Oh
no,' she said. 'I don't think there's any need to call in
Rhonda,' and she had Mary Lou give the upstairs a lick
and a promise. Now Eunice Stockbridge had her faults
but scrimpiness," she told him, giving the word full fla-
vor as she rolled it over her tongue, "scrimpiness was not
one of them."

"What time did you get home last night, Mrs. Stroud?"

"Eight o'clock. One hour late. Wayne drove me."

Mary Lou reappeared with the announcement that
Lance was on his way, her father was waking Paul, and
her mother was dressing. Right on cue thumping footsteps resounded on the back stairs and Lance popped into
the room. He had pulled on a sweatshirt and a pair of
jeans but looked unwashed and uncombed.

"Jeez, I'm sorry," he said, focusing on Mrs. Stroud,
who acknowledged this sentiment with a curt nod.

"Sit down, please, Mr. Turnbull," Sergeant Putnam
directed him. Lance swung himself jauntily into a
chair, grinning at his cousin, who was refreshing herself
with a stale breakfast roll. Mrs. Stroud attacked the
dishes in the sink with unusual vigor, making the china
rattle.

"Could you tell me, please, where you were last night
and what you were doing."

"Last night, last night," Lance mused as though five
years had passed. "What did we do last night, Lou?"

"I vacuumed."

"Oh, that's right. Old Lou was shoving the Hoover
around so I took the mater out for a treat. She's been
kinda down," he told Sergeant Putnam solicitously. "We
went to that ice cream stand over near Mount Pleasant

that has the pink-and-white-striped roof and twenty-
seven flavors, all natural ingredients. I had the double
dutch chocolate and Ma had the macadamia nut. You
hear that, Lou? That's one of Lou's favorites," he told
Sergeant Putnam with a grin. "She has about ten favorites. Well, then I brought her home and Lou was scrubbing toilets so I went out again, over to Bristol for a
six-pack and when I came home Lou had gone to bed, so
what the hell, I went, too."

"Anybody up when you got in?"

"Only my Uncle Avery and I rolled him, I mean I
helped him, to his room."

"What time was this?"

"About ten-thirty . . . yeah, about ten-thirty. Embar-
rassing to admit I went to bed at ten-thirty but when in
the sticks . . ."

"Did you notice if Wayne's car was in the garage?"

"You mean Graunty's Buick?" Lance answered slyly.

"I'm sorry, you're right. It doesn't belong to Wayne
yet, does it?"

A particularly loud crash took place at the sink as Lance
replied, "No, it doesn't and it wasn't and Paul was out,
too."

Sergeant Putnam, who had forgotten all about Avery
Stockbridge, sent Lance to awaken him while he spoke
with Henry and Ellen, who had gone to bed at ten
o'clock after an evening of solitaire and reading, re-
spectively, and hadn't heard a sound until the dawn's
early light evoked the chirping of sparrows outside
their windows. Avery's statement was not worthy of the
long wait he endured to obtain it as it quickly became
apparent that Avery had noticed nothing from eight
o'clock on. He recounted in meticulous detail his activities during the afternoon, which were entirely irrelevant to the inquiry, then poured himself a cup of coffee

and shuffled out of sight in the general direction of the dining room.

Paul, in contrast to his nephew, took time to shower and shave, but a fresh facade did not disguise the shadows under his eyes. Where had he gone last night when he left the station? He had started for Vangie's house in Weston, he admitted to Sergeant Putnam with a wry smile, had gone half the distance before he realized the folly of his venture, at which point he'd turned around, had a bite at a McDonald's and come straight home, arriving about eleven. He'd gone right to bed, feeling very low.

"Was everyone else here when you came in?"

"How would I know?"

"You might have noticed whose cars were in the yard. Had your cousin Malcolm arrived?"

"I think so."

"Lance here?"

"Yes."

"How about the Buick?"

"Yes. No, wait. I don't know. Hell, I didn't look at the cars."

"See anyone on your way in? Notice anything unusual?"

"As a matter of fact, there was a car ahead of me on the lake road, a green Ford, but I don't know if you'd call that unusual. It was probably someone from one of the cottages."

"Did you see the driver?"

"It was a man, alone, but that's all I could tell in the dark."

"Thank you, Paul, that's all for now."

He closed his notebook and stood up, leaving Paul surprised, as though he had expected something more. Mrs. Stroud plunked a mug of coffee down on the table in front of him and he began to stir it automatically.

"That green car," he said. "I just remembered. It had a bumper sticker on the back, 'Save a Tree: Eat a Beaver.'"

"I'll make a note of it."

He bade Mrs. Stroud farewell and went out the back door to find two state troopers methodically examining the Stockbridge vehicles, one by one, while Wayne stood grimly by.

chapter SIXTEEN

"Of course he's thought of hit and run, with that kind of bruising," said Chief Henderson, brushing powdered sugar off his tie. He had returned from the inquest to a midmorning cup of drugstore coffee and a packaged doughnut and was making use of this cozy interlude to compare notes with his sergeant.

Murder by person or persons unknown was the verdict at the inquest, thus putting a formal seal on their original diagnosis.

"Walfield very adroitly extracted from me every scrap of information we've gathered."

"Why? Does he think the two deaths are related?"

"He thinks this is a good chance to sneak back into the Eunice Stockbridge case, that's what he thinks. You get anything useful this morning?"

"I don't know," Sergeant Putnam said, pulling out his notebook. "If Walfield is looking for a hit-and-run driver, there are quite a few possibilities right at Pineacres. Lance was out last night at the right time, Paul, Wayne, any one of them could qualify. Lance's father arrived about quarter of ten; that might be a little early."

"Get those notes written up and I'll whisk them over to Walfield and then let's put our collective energies to work on our own case. I've been thinking, Dave, since I got back, and what I've been thinking about is Leon Stroud. I think we've got to know more about Leon Stroud. Why was he hanging around Pineacres? Where has he been since his release? Who has he seen? I suggest we start tracing Leon Stroud's movements immediately, and while I organize that little task I want you to take care of this: Miss Murchison heard noises in her yard again last night."

Sergeant Putnam groaned.

"She says there's a man's footprint under the kitchen window."

"Probably the meter reader."

"And our little arsonist is once more busy at the junior high, set fire to a roll of toilet paper this morning in the girls' bathroom."

"I'll go up to the school."

"You'll do both," said Chief Henderson firmly. "Ted is on a dog case. Why does everything descend on us at once?"

Sergeant Putnam went conscientiously through the motions of duty but his mind was whirling with images of Strouds and Stockbridges. Something seemed important; something had eluded him. If he could only stop and concentrate his mental efforts on the growing collection of disconnected facts that were accumulating in his head, perhaps he could form some coherent whole, trace some contiguous thread.

Miss Murchison asked him quaveringly in her thin old voice if he thought she ought to buy an attack dog and over at the junior high the administration was solemnly discussing the formation of squads of trained students with semipolice powers. What the hell was the matter with the world that force sprang so quickly to mind as the antidote to fear and frustration? Ted's view of humanity was little brighter, his canine client having died an agonizing death from the ingestion of poisoned pork chops.

In glum brotherhood they ascended the station stairs to encounter Chief Henderson popping wide-eyed out of his office with the announcement that Lance Turnbull had been arrested on charges of vehicular homicide. The state police had discovered a dent and a scratch on the fender of Lance's Mustang, the dent corresponding to injuries on Leon Stroud's body and the scratch presumably inflicted by the heavy signet ring he wore on his left hand. They had found dried lake mud on the floor of the car, beneath both driver's and passenger's seats, and they had come up with two witnesses to the presence of the Mustang on the lake road within the estimated time limits.

"Fellow taking his dog out saw the car pass about eleven-thirty going toward the end of the lake and a lady up with her baby went out to a porch rocker and saw it returning three-quarters of an hour later, going very fast, by the way. Wouldn't you know Walfield would get the cut-and-dried case, bing bang, all over in a day and we're still going nowhere."

"No question about the cause of death?"

"My God, no, Dave. He not only hit him, he went right over him and back again, dragged the body into the car, drove down to the end of the lake road and dumped Stroud into the water. Stupid really. He must have panicked."

Sergeant Putnam's heart felt as heavy as a lump of lead. He thought sadly of Louise and Malcolm Turnbull and their heartache. His concern went always to the parents in a case like this, being himself a parent and painfully aware of the precariousness of the position. And then he thought of Lance. Could anyone who had run over a man the night before appear as cocky and carefree as Lance had appeared that morning?

"He's a troublemaker," Chief Henderson said, not without a certain satisfaction, the facts confirming as they did his own initial impression. "Petty theft, car theft, some kind of drug problem. Not good material. But, God, what a blow to the family."

"Bea said to me the other day that the Stockbridges have had their sorrows. I guess she was more right than she knew."

"Oh Lord, speaking of Bea, she left a message for you, Dave; went clear out of my head. Said to tell you she's at Noreen Stroud's and you should come out there right away. Said you'd know what it was all about. Do you? What's she up to now?" he demanded with well-justified suspicion. "Not messing in this case, is she?"

"Not that I know of. She's been damned circumspect."

"Well, go ahead, then. But for God's sake, keep your wits about you."

Sergeant Putnam shed his jacket in respect to the midday sun and for the second time in two days drove out to Dogtown. The same scruffy wolf pack announced his arrival; the same grubby children poured out of the shacks in answer to the cacophony. The dogs, encountered without Ted's soothing presence, appeared frankly predacious, and he detected a certain shrill note creeping into his commands. The opening of the Strouds' front door prevented what might have been a humiliating scenario, an undignified scramble for the cruiser perhaps or some panicky flailing about with his cap.

Bea appeared tidy and cool in a lavender-and-white-checked sleeveless cotton dress and a pair of white plastic sandals with which she annually replaced her black basketball sneakers on the first of June. However cheerful her greeting, she avoided meeting his eyes, which made him certain that she was, as Len suspected, wholeheartedly messing in the case.

"Come in, David. Here he is, Noreen. Noreen and I have just had a bite of lunch."

Sergeant Putnam smiled to himself to see how completely Bea had taken over the kitchen, but Noreen seemed to have benefited from Bea's ministrations. She was sitting where he had left her, enveloped in a faded flowered wrapper; half a tuna-fish sandwich reposed on a plate in front of her. Sugar bowl, creamer, a dish of pickles, a tin of brownies, all spoke to him eloquently of Bea's approach. Maybe he and Len could take a lesson, although it was hard to picture them effectively employing Bea's gastronomic methods in the inhospitable aura of the station house.

He declined Bea's offer of a cup of tea; his shirt was sticking to his armpits. This little house must heat up like an oven during the summer, its yard devoid as it was of shade trees to block the sun's rays, or conversely, to act as a windbreak in the winter months when he pictured gales sweeping over the exposed plain, driving icy fingers through the cracks in the uninsulated walls. He was beginning to appreciate a little better Estelle Stroud's lack of levity.

"How are you, Noreen?" he asked her, taking a seat.

Noreen sniffed a couple of times and when she looked up, he saw traces of tears on her swollen cheeks.

"She's told me such a sad story," said Bea, shaking her head in commiseration and flashing him a glance of conspiracy. Clearly this was not the time to delve into the prologue to Bea's appearance in Noreen's house. Surely she hadn't ridden her bicycle five miles from Hampford Center. And how had she explained her arrival? Nobody just "passed by" Dogtown. Was she off at the same tangent he was, or had her thinking paralleled Len's so that she saw Leon Stroud as the key to the mystery? She had a way of being one jump ahead of them all.

"Did you know that your brother-in-law . . ." he began gingerly, feeling out the situation.

". . . that he's dead?" finished Noreen harshly. "I'm glad he's dead."

"She's glad he's dead," Bea explained, "because she hated and feared him and when he showed up again, out of prison, she was frightened all over again. But she's very upset because he died without telling her where he took her baby."

"Perhaps if you just started at the beginning . . ."

"I was just a girl," snuffled Noreen, her voice thickening. She stopped to take a sip of tea, holding the cup with a hand that trembled.

"Now don't you get yourself worked up again, Noreen, or your breathing will suffer. Why don't you eat that other half of your sandwich and drink your tea and I'll tell David the story you told me and you correct me if I'm mistaken at any point."

"All right, Miss Lambert."

"It started, David, when Leon Stroud married Estelle and they came to live here with her mother and grandmother and little sister Noreen. Noreen was only thirteen years old but her brother-in-law would not leave her alone, if you know what I mean."

She cast him a look brimming with significance and he found himself nodding solemnly back.

"He said he would kill her if she told anyone that he was touching her and she believed him and was very frightened of him as well as *repelled*," said Bea, who had a habit of underlining words as she spoke. "This went on for over a year and in the end, as you might guess, he *had his way*."

"Do you mean to tell me your sister knew nothing about this?"

"Not until I was pregnant," sniffed Noreen. "Then everybody knew."

"Go on, Bea."

"Well, she had the baby, a little boy, on March 4, 1955."

"I know."

"How?" demanded Noreen, startled.

"The information turned up during our investigation into Mrs. Stockbridge's death, Noreen. While looking through the county birth records, Officer Deegan discovered quite by accident that your baby was born just ten days before Paul Stockbridge."

Bea was doing funny things with her eyebrows.

"You don't think . . ." she murmured, eyes agleam; he cut her off with a frown and shook his head. Noreen had obviously not grasped the possible significance of his disclosure.

"He took my little baby," she said sadly. "He stole it from me."

"You see, she kept the baby," said Bea. "She found she wanted that little boy. She named him Ronald and brought him home. And one day Leon Stroud just took him away; Noreen never saw him again."

"What did he tell you he'd done with the baby?"

"He said he'd found a good home for him, a much better home than we could give him. Maybe that was true, but he was my little boy and he didn't . . . he didn't have the right . . ."

Tears cascaded down her cheeks, several plunking into her teacup. Bea reached across the table and took Noreen's heavy hand in her own thin fingers.

"I never had another baby," sobbed Noreen. "I don't know what happened, but I never had another one."

"And he didn't tell anyone where he placed the baby?"

"He never told me and he never told Estelle. I begged him, I told him I'd go to the police, I'd get a lawyer. He said he'd carve me up if I said a word and he would have, you know. He used to hit me all the time. He hit Estelle,

he hit the children. We were glad when he went to prison
for a long time. And then, about ten days ago, I saw him
in the middle of the night; he came to Grandma's window. He didn't see me. I didn't tell my sister. I wasn't
sure at first that it was him, but now I know it was. I was
frightened all over again. It was like a nightmare seeing
him standing there."

"He can't hurt you now," Bea said comfortingly.

"But you see," said Noreen, raising her wet face, "now
I'll never know what happened to Ronald."

"I'm not so sure about that," Sergeant Putnam told
her. "I think there's a good chance that you'll know what
happened to Ronald. Would it be okay if I had a word
with your grandmother?"

"Sure, go ahead," sniffed Noreen, and he left her to
Bea's hand patting and went down the tiny hallway and
knocked on the door frame of Augusta Belknap's room.
She eyed him from her nest of pillows with all the
warmth of a snake. He sat down without invitation on
the end of the bed and looked straight into her opaque
shoe-button eyes.

"A long time ago," he said, "Noreen had a baby. That
baby was fathered by Leon Stroud, Estelle's husband.
Leon and you sold that baby to the Stockbridges, who
raised him as their son."

She made an impatient movement with her bony little
claw as though dismissing trivia.

"I'm sure you and Leon were well paid for your services. Who was the intermediary? Who did you get to
approach the Stockbridges? They never knew whose
baby it was, did they?"

"Go away," she said in a cracked hoarse voice. "Get
out of here."

But her animosity lacked heart and he wondered how
much of a blow had been dealt to her by the death of

Leon Stroud. Surely a bond had existed between them, positive or negative, if he had been making her clandestine visits.

"Get out of my house," she said, but she was diminished, just a shrunken, very old woman who would take to her grave whatever she knew of Paul's adoption and Leon Stroud's death.

*   *   *

Sergeant Putnam gave Bea a ride back to Hampford. She'd come out, it transpired, on a Scooter Rooter truck driven by a local boy, on his way back to Mount Pleasant after a village emergency.

"I used my local history excuse," said Bea, "and don't look at me like that just because I haven't written it down yet; the day will come. We talked a bit about Dogtown and then I edged things on to a more personal level. She had just heard about Leon Stroud, poor thing, and it took but a few words to prime the pump."

He told her, in turn, that Lance Turnbull had been arrested for the hit-and-run death of Leon Stroud and Bea asked what Leon Stroud was doing down on the lake road late at night if he was not up to some mischief.

"You're very hard on the man, Bea. Isn't it possible he was hanging around Pineacres just to catch a glimpse of Paul?"

"Hah," said Bea, "you don't believe that any more than I do. A man who sells his child is not a sentimentalist."

She declined a ride to her doorstep, declaring she had errands downtown, but somehow when he pulled into the station parking lot, Bea was still with him, dogging his steps as he mounted the stairs. Chief Henderson was too impatient to impart his own news to bother with Bea in the first rush from his office.

"Listen to this, Dave; if this isn't the goddamnedest, excuse me, Bea, thing you ever heard. Mary Lou Stock-bridge marched into Walfield's office about an hour ago and told him he'd got the wrong man. She said she was sorry to frustrate his enthusiasm but she could not stand idly by while injustice triumphed. Or words to that effect. Anyway, it seems she knew that Paul was down at the lake, too, last night, something to do with mud on the stairs, and then she heard him lie to you this morning about the time he came in and then he told you some story about a green car . . ."

"He made a slip," said Sergeant Putnam, "about the Buick, said it was in the garage when it wasn't, but of course the second time he came it was. He *did* go out again. And then because he thought I caught his mistake, he fed me that cock-and-bull story about a green car with a male driver."

"That story," said Chief Henderson. "Mary Lou says that story is proof of his guilt. He wouldn't have provided a suspect unless he knew you were looking for a murderer and if he knew that, he knew that Leon Stroud didn't drown."

"Oh God, she's right. It's all beginning to fit together. Listen, Len, I'm going right down there. I'll explain when I get back."

"Now wait a minute, Dave," Chief Henderson called plaintively, but Sergeant Putnam was running down the stairs.

"Would you like me to fill you in, Len, while we're waiting?" Bea asked complacently.

chapter SEVENTEEN

Paul was seated in a small, square, white-walled room at the back of the state police barracks on Route 117 in Fordham. The room was stuffy, being windowless, but brightly lighted and furnished with a desk on which sat a tape recorder, a table, at which sat a sergeant, and a number of straight chairs, one of which contained Paul and another Walfield. Paul looked as though he had just played five sets of tennis on a jungle court; Walfield, in contrast, was as crisp and collected as ever and not at all displeased to have Sergeant Putnam appear at this particular moment of satisfaction. The outcome of Paul's interrogation had obviously more than offset whatever discomfiture he might have suffered at Lance Turnbull's reprieve.

"All wrapped up, Sergeant," he said somewhat smugly. "Mr. Stockbridge has confessed to accidentally striking and killing Leon Stroud last night with his nephew's Mustang. His fiancée apparently broke their engagement yesterday afternoon and in a state of depression, Mr. Stockbridge went down to meditate by the shore, taking Mr. Turnbull's car rather than subject his Corvette to the potholes. On his way home, rounding a corner, he came upon Leon Stroud walking in the middle of the road without a light; he struck him, he says, before he really saw him. After the accident, by his own admission, he lost his head and behaved with great stupidity.

He attributes his actions to shock," said Lieutenant Walfield coldly, the curl of his lip indicating his opinion of shock as an excuse for Paul's callous egotism.

"I think there's a little more to it than that," Sergeant Putnam said pleasantly, pulling up a chair. "Leon Stroud was your father, wasn't he, Paul?"

The intensity of Paul's reaction surprised him as much as it did Walfield, for Paul gave an agonized cry, buried his face in his hands, and burst into tears.

"Just what the hell is going on?" Walfield demanded, narrow-eyed, but Sergeant Putnam, leaning toward Paul, did not hear him.

"C'mon, Paul," he coaxed, "it's not as bad as that."

"Not as bad," Paul ground out. "He . . . he . . ."

"When did you find out?"

"Last night."

The words came muffled from behind his hands.

"When I went into the house the phone was ringing. I found out later that he'd been watching for me; he called from Wayne's apartment."

"What time?"

"About eleven. I did start for Vangie's when I left you and then I turned back just like I told you."

He let his hands drop and stared bleakly at the floor; his tears, a reaction to shock, had stopped as abruptly as they began.

"So you answered the phone and he said what?"

"He said, 'Paul?' and I said, 'Yes,' and he said, 'This is your father calling.' I thought it was a prank and I laughed and I said, 'The joke's on you, sucker; my father's dead.' Then he said, 'No, he isn't. I'm your father and I want to see you.' Well, I started to shake. I mean, I thought for twenty-eight years that my father was dead and here is this guy telling me he's alive. He asked me to meet him in half an hour at the far end of the lake beyond

159

the houses where it gets marshy. There's a road there off the lake road that leads to an old landing where they used to put canoes in, but it's all overgrown with water plants and unused now. So I said I'd meet him and I just sat there in the hall for fifteen or twenty minutes and I *was* in shock, believe me. I never wondered why he wanted to meet me at night or in that particular spot or where he had been all these years. The only thing that went through my mind, over and over, was the fact that this man with a hoarse voice said he was my father."

"So I went to meet him. I didn't want to take my car down there, the road is one big rut, so I took Lance's. He keeps a spare key under the seat."

How casually, thought Sergeant Putnam, did he use and discard other people's property, and this attitude of fine disregard toward material possessions defined to Sergeant Putnam, more than any other trait, his social class.

"And then I got down there and I waited around a bit and it was dark as hell except for the moonlight and kind of spooky and, God, I was so nervous and it occurred to me that it might be a hoax, a sick joke, and I was just about convinced it was when suddenly there's this guy coming out of the woods. He was a scruffy bastard," he told them, the shock still vivid enough to cause a tremor in his voice, "a scruffy little fat man, unshaven, wearing a dirty T-shirt and he told me *he* was my father. He told me he was Mrs. Stroud's husband and her sister was my mother. And all the time he was telling me this, he kept eyeing me up and down as though he were judging me, like I was some kind of possession. And I guess he approved of what he saw because he kept grinning, and then he told me that he and this old lady . . ."

"Her name is Augusta Belknap. She's your great-grandmother."

"How do you know about her?"

"I've just been to see her, Paul, and your mother also."

"My mother." Paul laughed bitterly, "Some half-witted Dogtown squaw . . ."

". . . who loves you very much and has never stopped grieving over your loss."

"Oh my God."

Once again Paul's head dropped forward, forehead to hand. Walfield, who had been following the exchange with growing interest, challenged Sergeant Putnam's imperturbable pace.

"What did Stroud tell you?"

Paul raised his head with a sigh.

"He said they planned it, the old lady and him. They planted me in that family like an investment. My parents were middle-aged; they could die when I was relatively young without surprising anyone. Then when I inherited everything, they would make their claim."

"They had no right to a penny of your inheritance if you were legally adopted," Lieutenant Walfield said scornfully. "You were, weren't you?"

"Yes, but it wasn't a legal claim, it was a moral one. They expected me to still be one of them. They expected me to be a Stroud and their willing gold mine and as gleeful as they were at putting one over on the Stockbridges. What he didn't count on was sitting in prison for eighteen years. And she had to wait with him, year after year, getting older and older. As soon as he was released he came rushing up here to cash in. He told me how he killed Mother," Paul cried, "as casually as though he were telling me about stepping on an ant, and he expected me to *applaud* him, that was the horrible thing. He kept grinning at me in that awful way he had, as though we were confederates. He told me how he stole one of those yellow robes from the Blossoms' cabin and walked

161

boldly right into the house and out again through the sun porch."

"Did he tell you why he picked an afternoon when the house was full of people?" Walfield asked him.

"Because of Wayne. If only Wayne and Mary Lou were at Pineacres when Mother died and there was any question of its not being a natural death, then suspicion would immediately fall on Wayne. Not that he expected anything to go wrong. He was so pleased with his cleverness that when I told him about the cosmetics on the pillowcase he shrugged it off as bad luck that Mary Lou should have noticed; he really didn't understand that he gave *himself* away, putting the pillow underneath like that. He was a stupid, evil, arrogant man and I told him I wouldn't have anything to do with him and that I was going to take the whole story to the police. And he just kept grinning and he said that blood was thicker than water and he'd give me twenty-four hours to get used to the idea of being a Stroud and then he'd meet me again in the same place. *Son,* he called me; 'I'll see you tomorrow, son.' And then he just turned and walked away along the side of the road.

"I got in the car, I was shaking like hell, I got in and started the engine and somehow the sight of him walking along so jauntily unleashed something terrible in me and I thought to myself, That man murdered Mother, that's all I could think of, he murdered her, and I drove right at him. I wanted to crush him. I hit him and I backed over him and I hit him again and then I just sat there and after a while I shoved him into the car. I thought I might go bury him somewhere in the woods but I couldn't stand being near him so I dragged him out again and down to the water and pushed him in. And I'll tell you something," he said fiercely, raising a contorted face, "I'm not sorry I did it. Under the same circumstances, I'd do it all over again."

"I wouldn't mention that in a courtroom," Lieutenant
Walfield cautioned him dryly.

"Paul," said Sergeant Putnam, rising to leave, "was it
Augusta who arranged the adoption?"

"My loving great-grandmother, yes," Paul said bitterly. "She was cook at Pineacres. She went to Mother
and told her about this girl who was in trouble and how
she couldn't afford to keep her baby but she just *happened*
to have this lawyer who could arrange everything. God
knows what it cost them altogether. The old lady and
Leon Stroud shared twenty thousand dollars. It's nice to
know what you're worth."

*　　*　　*

Sergeant Putnam, on his return to the station, found Bea
and Chief Henderson keeping vigil in Len's smoke-
fogged office. Ash was sprinkled liberally across Chief
Henderson's shirt front, tie, and desk, and he greeted Sergeant Putnam with a bellowing cough. Bea's thin face
peered eagerly at him through the haze.

"Did he do it, David?"

"He did. He killed his father."

"Oh my gracious." But she shook her head in sorrow
rather than surprise. Very little in human nature caught
Bea by surprise anymore.

"He proved himself a Stroud in the end," she said, as
the tale unfolded. "*Backing over his father;* what a thin ve-
neer of social graces the boy had! Heredity will out, that's
been my experience. Don't you remember the Wimble
boy, Len, who proved such a sad trial to the poor Wimbles with his everlasting deviltry? One day, David, his
birth mother appeared on the porch larded with makeup,
in a satin dress, and he got into her big car and went off
with her just like that."

"Much to the relief of the Wimbles, I should think,"

163

said Sergeant Putnam, but Bea sighed and said, "After all they had done for him."

"I'll tell you frankly, Bea, I don't think it was the Stroud in Paul but the Stockbridge that caused the trouble. I think it was the discovery of his parents' lowly origin that brought him to such an emotional state. I might even go so far as to say that this is the first murder I've ever come across in which the motive was snobbery."

"It does make you wonder," Chief Henderson agreed, "whether he was overcome with emotion or cold calculation. Leon Stroud, as you say, was a tremendous liability to a man in Paul's position. Don't you think that fact might have occurred to Paul as he saw Stroud walking away, that the fellow had a pretty heavy hold over him whether he played along or not?"

"I would rather believe that he was overcome with grief for Eunice," Bea said firmly, "and I am sure any jury when they hear this sordid tale will let him off lightly. But, my goodness me, what a sad mess for the family."

"By God, I can't believe it's all cleared up so quickly," Chief Henderson told them, looking anything but sad. "I was gearing up for a long slog and here we are basking in glory, thanks to a lot of stupidity. Not yours," he hastened to assure Sergeant Putnam. "I mean Paul being as careless as his father. Maybe *that's* a family trait, and good for us if it is. Why don't you skip out early, Dave, and spend some well-earned time with the kids? I'm just going to sit here and feel happy. Oh, by the way, our pal from the Blossoms called while you were out, what's-his-name, Arthritis."

"Adoram. What did he want?"

"Wanted to let us know that they *did* see Henry Stockbridge skulking around the cabin last Friday afternoon. I told him he was three reels behind but thanks anyway."

"Good God." Sergeant Putnam laughed. "Talk about cautious. I suppose it's a habit ingrained by a certain amount of persecution."

"Well, off you go, Dave. You go with him, Bea. It sticks in my throat to thank you, but I suppose I ought to."

"Any tiny contributions I can make, as an alert citizen, to the general good," said Bea smoothly, as she stood, "I consider it my duty to make. There is no call to thank me for upholding my civic responsibility."

And bestowing a regal nod upon Chief Henderson, she made her exit on Sergeant Putnam's arm. He drove her home up Prince's Lane to a yard that was drenched with the scent of honeysuckle and early roses.

"My goodness, I'm not in the mood to scrub my kitchen floor."

Bea's last words, delivered as she gathered up purse and gloves, remained with him while he parked the cruiser and set off across the common toward Summer Street. No more was he able to slip back easily into everyday life, after the heightened emotion of the past few days. He greeted, therefore, with surprised relief, the discovery in his kitchen of a visitor who could afford him the luxury of a transitional phase. Mary Lou, in her god-awful shorts, was drinking iced tea and eating brownies at the kitchen table with Barbara, while Jenny played happily on the floor with a large book of hydrocephalic paper-doll babies.

"Look what Mary Lou brought me, Daddy," she exclaimed, holding up one of the grinning infants, and Mary Lou blushed, mortified that he might think she was bribing her way into friendship. He hung his jacket and cap on a chair and joined the women, accepting a glass of iced tea gratefully. Then leaning back, refreshed, he told them Paul's story.

"Do you mean that he was going to let Lance take the blame?" asked Barbara indignantly.

"I'm afraid he was. Although, in all fairness, we don't know how far he would have gone if Mary Lou hadn't spoken up, whether, for instance, he would have let Lance go to prison for him if it reached that point."

"Oh, he would have," said Mary Lou. "Paul is used to using people. He considers Lance expendable."

"Why, that's awful."

"It is, isn't it? But Paul is Graunty's creation. There's something hollow at the core. Poor Lance, not one of them even *questioned* his guilt. Aunt Louise wrung her hands and said, 'How could he do this to us?' and, 'Where did we go wrong?' and Uncle Malcolm was running around trying to reach the right connections and Uncle Avery thought he was a fool to get caught, and my mother said she had been expecting something like this since Lance was two years old. But it wasn't at all what anyone should have expected from Lance."

"How about Lance himself? How did he feel?"

"About Paul's betrayal? He said, 'Shoddy way to treat a nephew, eh, what?' "

Sergeant Putnam grinned with her.

"What will happen to you when the story comes out?"

"To the family as a whole? It will hardly cause a tremor. Paul is not a true Stockbridge, don't you see; he simply reverted to type. There may be some fleeting satisfaction in some quarters at the family's embarrassment but it won't last long. I mean, my Lord, old families are practiced in weathering scandal; if they weren't, there wouldn't be a single one left.

"Lance is going to use his money to go to California," Mary Lou told them, absentmindedly appropriating the last brownie. "Uncle Avery will drink his up. My mother and the old man are going to do some traveling which will be nice for them. He's very restless, you know, being a man of action, and she can daub Italian landscapes as well as New England ones. Uncle Malcolm, I suppose, will feel called upon to make some splashy, holy gesture like endowing a string of retreat houses or a hundred dusty missions and Aunt Louise, who has got to face the fact that she had no faith in her son, is going to be in a debasing mood and will agree with him and then when their car breaks down or they go into the rectory's drafty bathroom some winter afternoon, they will secretly regret their largess and turn bitter in their old age. As for Pineacres, perhaps it's time to let it go. Perhaps it's not meant to be a twentieth-century house."

It was only an hour later, after Mary Lou had left, that it occurred to Sergeant Putnam that he had heard everyone's plans but hers. He sought out Barbara, who was cutting up string beans for supper and enfolded her in his arms from behind.

"Didn't she tell you, Dave? Why, she's going to take her ten thousand and open a home for abandoned dogs. And she says she owes the whole idea to me!"